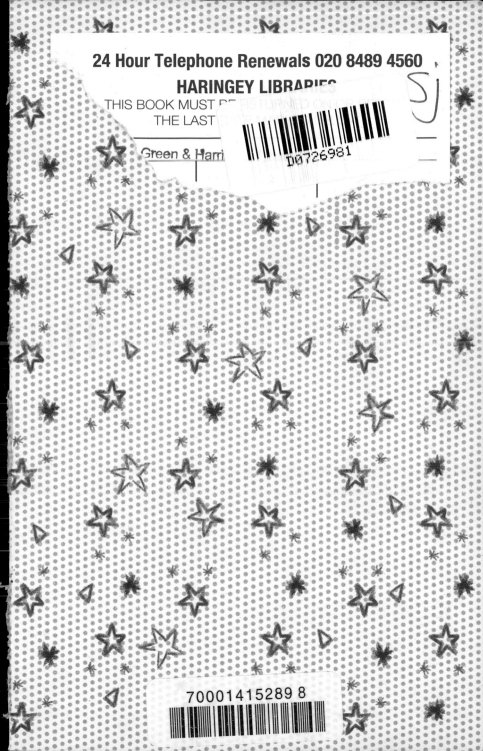

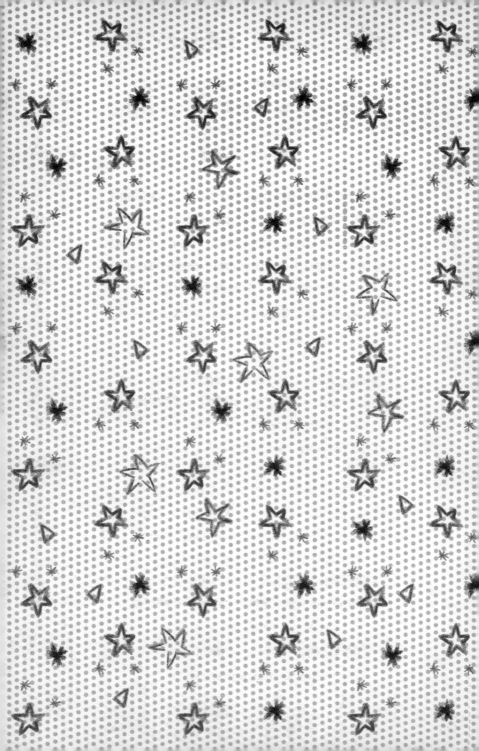

HARRY HEAPE is an artist, a visionary and a very successful none-of-your-businessman. A shy and quiet man, Harry lives and writes on the edge of a magical forest where he spends any spare time that he has collecting pine cones and volunteering at his local monkey prison.

REBECCA BAGLEY lives in Bath (the city, not A BATH, although she did have one once) where she draws pictures so she doesn't have to get a real job. When she's not hanging out in the world of children's books, she'll probably be in a headstand, plotting how to best smuggle a husky into her flat without anyone noticing.

Shiny Pippin
and the
Broken Frest

Harry Heape

Illustrated by
Rebecca Bagley

ff

FABER & FABER

First published in 2018
by Faber and Faber Limited
Bloomsbury House, 74–77 Great Russell Street,
London WC1B 3DA

Typeset in Caslon by M Rules
Printed and bound by
CPI Group (UK) Ltd, Croydon CR0 4YY

A CIP record for this book
is available from the British Library

ISBN 978–0–571–33215–1

FSC
www.fsc.org
MIX
Paper from
responsible sources
FSC® C101712

1 3 5 7 9 10 8 6 4 2

For E, L, R and C,

with all my love.

HH

x

Twinkle, Twinkle, Little Star

Permit me, lovely readers, to take you back in time. Firstly though, wherever you are, it is important that you should be comfy. For example, if you are in bed, make sure there are no spiky pieces of Lego under your bum-bum.

That sort of thing simply won't do. Okay? Great. Now close your eyes, breathe deeply and open them again very slowly. Are you ready? Good, then let us begin.

Many years ago, high in the night sky, a little old star flew through a distant galaxy. Once it had been a brilliant star, the most fantastic in the whole sky – a star bursting with *magical possibilities*.

Now the star was ten trillion years old and it knew that it was dying. It had sped past planets and weaved in and out of constellations for a year and a day, until it was no bigger than a cauliflower.

It wanted somewhere beautiful to die,

somewhere it could pass on its magic. Finally it spotted our little blue planet and it felt instinctively that this was the perfect place.

It hurtled towards the ground, intent on crashing into a hillside and burying its powers deep within the soil. A farmer saying goodnight to his animals watched it streaking above his home.

By the time it saw the edge of the forest, the little star knew it wouldn't make it to the ground. So it self-destructed and exploded in a shower of very special, shimmering sparkles, which cascaded onto the hillsides and surrounding forest.

The sparkles rained down on the farmer's

little cottage, where his wife and twin baby children slept. They drifted down the chimney and they fizzed and flickered and bounced through each of the rooms. Outside, all was quiet – until a little bird began to sing.

Over time, the star's magic did soak deep into the soil and the farmhouse, where it waited and it waited. A great many years later, this twinkly, shiny, brilliant magic had grown into something rather wonderful and this, my lovely readers, is what our story is all about.

Granny's House

ow, my fabulous friends, let me introduce you to the hero of our story. Her name is Pippin. She is not one of those super-confident heroes you read about in other books. She is just a little girl who loves her mum and dad and her granny and her pet mouse, Tony. Her hobbies are making snowmen, playing the recorder and colouring in. She lives in a pretty little town called Funsprings, which perches on a steep-sided valley on the edge of a magical forest.

So the day our story begins, Pippin was at her granny's. Pippin spent a great deal of her time at her Granny Margaret's because her mum and dad were ALWAYS busy, busy, busy but NOT quite as busy as Pippin, who was ALWAYS busy, busy, busy, busy, busy, busy, busy.

She was at her granny's that very morning, with Tony snuggling in her shirt pocket and a huge smile on her face. Her eyeballs were alive with sparkles of excitement, because her granny had just bought an enormous television.

'Grandmama, wow, what a massive new tellywision you've got!' she shrieked.

'All the better for watching the snooker,'
said Granny. 'Let's stick it on and do some
sofa snuggling,' she added with an ancient
twinkle in her one working eye. (Granny's

other eye was always covered with an eye patch. Sometimes the little old lady told Pippin that she'd lost it whilst battling an evil scientist on top of a fast-moving train. Other times she told Pippin that her eyeball was in the tummy of a crocodile somewhere on the Zambezi River. Whether any of these stories were true or not didn't matter – it was exactly this sort of special funusual nonsense that made Pippin adore her granny.)

So the two of them snuggled down on the sofa and gazed at the enormous television. Snooker's most ridiculous star, Donnio Sillyman, was about to play his shot with a fishing rod when . . . the picture suddenly disappeared and an anxious-looking news reporter came on!

Granny and Pippin edged closer to the screen. They could see that the reporter was standing in a very familiar square, next to a very familiar fountain, which was blowing very UNfamiliar sand into a very familiar sky.

'Hello everybody! I'm in Funsprings, where, as you clever viewers know, it hasn't rained for **A YEAR** and all the rivers and streams and lakes have dried up. Well, if that wasn't bad enough, guess what – the famous fun springs of Funsprings have just run out of water! Biologists, geologists, meteorologists and all the other ologists are badly baffled and completely

11

confused. Viewers, this is all very serious.'

Granny got up and switched off the TV. 'So all the water has officially gone,' she sighed. Her twinkliness took on a sadder, bluer tone. 'Pippin, I have been very worried about this. What about all the poor woodland creatures? The hedgehogs? The rabbits? My goodness, what about the beautiful deer? We must do something to help them, but I am way too old and wiggly to nonsense around in the forest.'

'Grangran!' Pippin said excitedly, jumping up and down like a constipated kangaroo. (Tony the mouse was boinged around so much inside her shirt pocket that he did six somersaults. Sometimes he wished his special friend didn't have *quite* so much energy.)

'What is it, my lovely?' asked Granny.

'I can be your legs! With your brains and my funergy we can do it, I'm sure,' said Pippin. 'We can bring the water back to Funsprings and then all the animals can drink and burp and dance in the sunshine again! What do you say, Granny? I can't do it on my own though. Say you'll help? P-LEASE?' she begged.

Granny looked at Pippin and smiled. 'You'd be surprised what things you can do on your own, my love . . . I think it is time to tell you something very important.' Her smile went away. 'Pippin, follow me, down to my cellar,' she said.

'I didn't know you had a smellar, Grangran!' grinned Pippin, with a hundred and ten kilograms of twinkliness in her tummy. Whenever Pippin had visited previously, the door had always been hidden – covered over with seventy-five aprons hanging on a hook.

These days Granny was a bit of a slow mover, so she asked for a piggywiggyback. Luckily for Pippin, tiny Granny was as light as a baby bird because she only ate marshmallows and Monster Munch and only ever drank the bubbles from lemonade.

'Ooh, Grangran, this is super-exciting!' said Pippin as she walked very carefully down the stairs, her little granny clamped on her back like a silver-haired fighter pilot landing a Pippin-shaped aeroplane.

At the bottom of the stairs, Granny climbed down and began searching for the light switch. After a few moments of a-fumbling and a-mumbling very rude phrases, which I can't possibly repeat (like 'bum factories' and 'potato snakes' – oops, I did. Tiny sozzikins everybody), she finally found the switch and turned on the light. And wow, Pippin's eyeballs nearly popped out and rolled under a cupboard, because what she saw was SO exciting and funusual.

Unfortunately for you, there is an ice-cream van outside my house and it is calling my name so I am going to leave the excitement for the next chapter and go and get a Cornetto. Big **sozzikins** but also yum-yum.

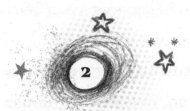

Goodness Gracious Crikey and Zoink-a-Doodle Jinkies

'Goodness gracious crikey and zoink-a-doodle jinkies!' exclaimed Pippin, wide-eyed. Granny's cellar looked like something from a

17

film – the headquarters of a superagent or a secret hero.

There were grappling hooks, crossbows, night-vision goggles, lots of armour-plated suits and in one corner was a motorbike that looked like it had been borrowed from Sir Geoffrey Motorbike, the inventor of very fast motorbikes.

Pippin raced around the cellar taking it all in. It was obvious the room had not been used for many years. All of the cool gadgetry was covered in a thick layer of dust and spidery webs of cob hung from every corner.

Tony the little mouse must have been able to feel Pippin's heart racing, because he popped his head out of her pocket and stared, open-mouthed, around the room.

'Wow times a hundred and nine wowzers!' said Pippin. 'But I don't funderstand, Grangran. What is all this? I'm confuzzled.'

'Well,' began Granny. 'All this nonsense is here because I used to have a special gift called Shinyness. I still have that gift but I am so old and dusty that it's not as much use to me now. But ages ago I used my gift to help people. I went on special missions to save the world from evil scientists and that sort of thing. I haven't spent the *whole* of my life on my bottom watching lovely snooker!'

Granny chuckled. 'But here's the important thing, Pippin: you have the same gift. You, my love, are Shiny, too.'

'Shiny, Grangran? Silver teapots and bald men's heads are shiny, not little girls!' replied Pippin, still gazing around her.

'This is a different sort of Shiny,' said Granny. 'This Shiny is a magical, gifty-wifty thing that grows out of kindness, light and love. You see, a hundred years ago a beautiful star died in this very forest and as it died it scattered the most amazing magic all around us. Magic that courses through you, my love and through many of the creatures around us, including little Tony.'

'How do you know about Tony, my very very very secret pet mouse?' Pippin asked her granny, shocked.

'It's because I Shine too, my little one, which means I know LOADS of stuff that's going on. I keep it secret like you do, but now I think it's high time you knew more about this Shiny magic because you must use it to find out why the water has gone away! You must go into the woods and talk with other animals! You must find out the truth!'

Sorry, my lovely readers – I should maybe have mentioned that Pippin and Tony could talk to each other, but it was a big secret for her and she made me cross my sniffconk and pinkie-promise not to say a thingy.

'Haha, Grancakes!' laughed Pippin. 'I can only talk to Tony. I'd be way too nervmouse to talk to another animal. I wouldn't even say boo to a gooseberry.'

Granny held Pippin's hand and looked into her twinkly brown eyes. 'I understand, you little muffin. That's because Tony is your first special Shiny friend, your soulmate. But, you will, in time, be able to talk with other animals – if your gift is allowed to grow. That's what's so good about being Shiny.'

Pippin looked at Granny open-mouthed.

She couldn't believe what she was hearing. 'Are you sure?' she asked.

'Confirmative.' Granny nodded with a smile.

'Cool!' said Pippin. 'It would be awesomething to talk to other animals and I would love it if Tony could talk to other people too. I'm sure he'd like that.'

(But I'm afraid to say, lovely readers, that inside Pippin's pocket, Tony wasn't so sure. He was a shy little mouse who loved cheese but hated change. 'I don't want you to talk to anyone else,' he said quietly to himself. But enough about him. Back to Pippin.)

Granny went on. 'There are two important

things about being Shiny. Not only can you talk to other animals, you can sometimes tell what they are thinking, too. Do you sometimes know what Tony is thinking, Pippin?'

Pippin was even more excited now. 'Yes, I do, Grangran! On the way to your house this morning he was thinking about Babybels, hazelnuts and dancing. He thinks about those sorts of things quite a lot.' Pippin paused for breath.

'So, Grangran, how do I learn to talk to other animals?' asked the little girl.

'Tony will help you,' Granny explained. 'That is one of the most important jobs of your special Shiny friend.'

'Oo, Tony, this is brill,' said Pippin, full of wonder, picking Tony up. But Tony pretended to be asleep – he didn't like what he was hearing AT ALL. So Pippin popped him back in her pocket and went back to talking to Granny, who was loads more fun than an asleep mouse.

'Who's YOUR Shiny friend, Grangran?' Pippin asked. 'Is she a wise old owl? I hope she IS an owl. I love owls. Is she a lobster? Is she a squirrel? I know she's not a jellyfish, is she, Gran?'

'I can tell you that my special friend is not a jellyfish or even a stick insect, for that matter!'

Pippin's mind skipped away from her granny's special friend. 'This is sooOOO exciting. I feel sparklier and brighter and more magical already. How do I begin talking to more animals, Gran, where do we start?'

'We start,' explained Granny, 'the way I always used to when I was planning my missions. With tea and biscuits!' She beamed. 'And then, if I wasn't a wobbly old goat that smelled of Lucozade and lavender, I'd go and investigate the Old Laboratory in Babbins Wood – the one that had the fire last year. That place has never *smelled right* to me.'

'Good planny, Granny!' Pippin twinkled.

They then gobbled some tea and biscuits.

After that, Granny gave Pippin a backpack full of useful things from her cellar to help with her mission. Among other things, it contained:

A walkie-talkie

A cat burglar's costume

Some swimming gogglers

A rubber chicken

A hard-boiled eggy-weg

Some dynamite

A rope

A bin liner

HELPFUL
TIE-UP bits

Pippin's favourite powerball

A pair of shorts

And a partridge in a pear tree

Haha! Not really that last one, my lovelies! That was just me mucking about like a monkey in a wig.

So, with a funny smell as her only clue, Pippin set off.

'You go and have fun.' The old lady smiled. 'See you back here for tea. We'll drink pink lemonade and munch Monster Munch until it comes out of our earholes.'

And with that, the little girl was gone.

But what Granny didn't know was that this was NOT going to be a gentle gladventure. This was going to be an incredibubbly scarifying and very dangerous badventure – the MOST scarifying and dangerous badventure that the forest had seen for MORE THAN FIFTY EARS!!!

Oswald

Out in the beautiful, sun-speckled forest of Funsprings, a herd of deer was walking quietly. They moved like a gentle brown train, in and out of shafts of soft sunlight, towards their morning drink. They looked magical. Sunbeams filtered through the trees and

danced on their adorable chocolatey-brown noses and made pretty patterns on their big podgy bum-bums.

The deer all looked very similar – all of them, that is, except for Oswald, their king. The big white stag was incredibubble, like something from a funbelievable dream. Enormous and as white as snow, he seemed as though he was from another time and place entirely.

His majestic coat bore the scars of seventy-seven battles and two enormous and very fighty wars. If you were ever lucky enough to glimpse Oswald in the forest, you might hide under a bush and telephone a police dog, saying that you had just seen a goats. Gaaah! Sorry. I mean a ghost!!!

King Oswald was at the rear of the procession. He was pretending to keep an eye on things, but really he was secretly planning his next snooze. You see, Oswald was tired. YOU'D be tired if you had fought in seventy-seven battles and two enormous and very fighty wars. So nowadays, the thing that Oswald liked doing most was relaxing.

At the front of the herd was Oswald's young son, Martin. Martin was the opposite of Oswald. He was bouncy, energetic and fast. If he had been a human, he would have been the sort of human that got up ever so early and said 'Right!' all the time.

Martin loved his father and he loved hearing of Oswald's badventures. He hoped that one day he would be as loved and respected as his father. Martin did a bit of the looking after of the herd, but Oswald was still very much numero uno, the head honcho with the biggest poncho.

Recently something had been troubling young Martin. As the deer walked, he sensed an opportunity to talk to his dad. It had been obvious for a while that something was wrong with the forest.

And he wasn't just talking about the lack
of water.

'Father,' Martin began. 'I feel that
there is something not quite right with the
forest's natural order. There seems to be
an imbalance—'

'An ambulance! Good heavens! Where?'
asked Oswald, looking up.

'No, father: an IMBALANCE,' Martin
continued. 'Something missing from our
world. Do you feel it too?'

Oswald didn't speak for quite a while.
They walked on, in and out of sunbeams
and then just as Martin was wondering
whether his father had in fact nodded off

and was actually sleepwalking, Oswald finally replied, 'Yes, son. There are, I think, TWO things that are wrong, but my mind is old and a little bit crusty and dusty and I am not sure exactly what they are.'

Martin was confuzzled and annoyed. How could his dad know that there were TWO things wrong but not know what they were?

By now the herd was passing close to the Old Laboratory. You could just see its burned and twisted metal roof through the trees. The deer were heading towards a deep pool, fed by an underground spring.

Before the rain and water had stopped, they'd been able to drink from the river or the many streams that ran through Babbins Wood. Now this place was the only spot for miles around that still had delicious, refreshing water. Oswald had found it, so the deer called it Oswald's Well. But they didn't like it much. It was too near the scary lavatory – gaaah. Silly me! I knew I would do that sooner or later – I do of course mean the scary *laboratory*.

'Oh, now I remember! That place is one of the forest's problems,' said King Oswald, looking at the lab. 'I've been having bad feelings about it for a long time. I don't know what's going on inside, but I sense dangerous danger and very high levels of dangerosity.'

Martin looked up at the spooky old laboratory. It made him do a shiver.

'The second thing, I think,' Oswald continued, 'is the imbalance you describe, son. I believe there's something wrong within the forest. At first I thought it was just because of the water going missing, but it's more than that ...'

'Do you think that the laboratory and the broken forest are connected, Papa?' Martin asked.

Oswald looked at Martin and nodded. 'I

most certainly do, son. The thing is, I have no idea how …'

The young stag looked at his father. He felt super-energised, like a brand new robot that had been on charge ALL NIGHT.

'Right!' Martin said. 'Drink long and hard, father and then let us run together, you and I. We will cover every inch of the forest and we'll find out exactly what is going on!'

'RUN?' spluttered Oswald, spitting out a huge mouthful of water. 'RUN? Are you out of your mind, my deer boy? I'm afraid my plan for today was to lump around as much as possible. Maybe sing a few verses of "Doe a Deer" somewhere nice and shady. You know I don't run any more. Running smells.'

Martin looked at his father. The old stag was beginning to get right up his nostrils. He wanted his dad to be the brave king of long ago. Martin was impatient: he needed action NOW, or even earlier than now if possible. For Martin, quarter-to-now would NOT be too early for action. Why should he wait, if all the old man wanted to do was snooze and sing and fart?

Oswald could see his son was about as fed up as a duck at a disco. Martin was desperate to take over from his father and lead the herd, but Oswald knew his son was not quite ready. However, thought Oswald to himself, the boy was quick and brave and they had to find out what was happening . . .

The king of the forest winked at the young deer and lovingly nudged him with his big white muzzle. 'I tell you what, Martin. YOU run. You like running; you're good at running. Meanwhile, I will get in touch with an old and very important friend. Then we'll put our heads together and see what we come up with. Deal-a-roony?'

'Deal-a-roony!' Martin grinned. 'Right!' he said again. 'Okay, so I think the best way to start would be to run along the dry riverbed ...'

But Oswald was only half listening. He'd spotted a stag-sized area of extremely comfy-looking moss underneath an oak tree and was imagining how super it would feel under his ancient bum-bum. 'That sounds great, son, off you pop,' he yawned.

As Martin hurtled into the woods, Oswald thought that he could allow himself just forty winks. He snuggled down and started to sing himself quietly to sleep ...

Dope. A deer. A female deer,
Yay, a drop of golden fun ...
Me, that's me, that's me, you know,
Mo Farah, a long, long way can run ...

A Different
Shine

Not very far away, Pippin was walking through the woods in the direction of the Old Laboratory, with Tony in her pocket. The sun was shining brightly and a soft breeze tickled the armpits of the trees and made them do gentle rustly giggling.

Tony tried to get everything straight in his head. Shininess was an ancient magic. Okay. It meant that Pippin could talk to animals, they could talk to her, not just him AND they could also communicate telepathically … And he could do it too!

THEN ALL OF A SUDDEN SOMETHING STRANGE BEGAN HAPPENING TO TONY.

The little mouse saw a vision of a beastly figure at a table. He looked like a mad scientist and was as tall and as spindly as a lamp post. Evil scientists are always skinny because they are too evil to eat. You never hear an evil scientist saying, 'Mmm, you know what? I really fancy a nice sandwich' OR 'let's go for some chips', do you? They are too busy being appalling, ghastly and mean.

Our poisonous professor wore a white lab coat, with a row of pens in the top pocket and a withered flower in the lapel. His slim trousers weren't quite long enough for him and he wore big pointy shoes on his evil feet. The man's face was not yet clear to Tony, but he had a mane of grey, swept-back hair and his hands were tiny and thin and looked like they belonged to an Egyptian mummy.

Slowly the little mouse realised what

was up – he was SHINING, but not with Pippin! For the first time in his life, Tony was Shining with somebody else – HE COULD TELEPATHICALLY SEE WHAT THEY WERE DOING! – and he didn't like it one little bit, thank you very much for asking.

The evil scientist lifted a telephone and spoke in a menacing whisper. 'If the diamond is not found soon, Gareth will be having baby mole for breakfast. Do I make myself clear?' As he put the phone down, a fat white cat jumped up onto the table and licked its lips. The ghastly gentleman now spoke to the cat. 'What am I, Gareth?'

'You are a genius, Dr Blowfart,' the cat purred.

'Yes, dear one,' the creature whispered. 'But what *kind* of genius am I?'

'A very naughty one,' replied the cat.

The figure rose shakily and made his way towards the cat. 'And what am I going to do now, Gareth?' he asked.

The cat looked up. 'I don't know, Master. But whatever you choose to do today, I have the feeling that it will be deliciously mean and frightfully rotten.'

Tony's scary Shine broke and he looked around himself again, bouncing gently in Pippin's shirt pocket, feeling shocked and scared.

But Pippin's mind was so full of questions about her own Shining, she didn't pick up that Tony was frightened. His little heart was pounding and he was petrified. Tony thought of the huge warmth and love that existed between them and the endless snuggly cuddles they enjoyed. It was the kind of love that made Tony feel nine feet tall. He could do with some of that now, he thought.

But as they continued through the woods, Pippin just kept yicketing on about her new powers. 'Oo, Tony, I love the idea of Shining with lots of other creatures. It's basically like a superpower. Talking to other animals would be great!'

NO IT FLIPPITY WOULDN'T, thought Tony.

Pippin stopped. This time she *had* read her mouse's little mind. She felt sad – she did want to talk to other animals, but she certainly didn't want to upset her beloved friend.

'I don't want you to talk to other animals,' Tony blurted out. 'Pippin, you're not some kind of magical hero, you're just a little girl who's being a nincompooping-crabby-muffin and you've made me want to go home.'

Now Pippin was angry. 'Well, that's just

mean of you, Tony. If you're not going to help me then maybe I'll leave you here on your own in the forest and go and find some friends who *aren't* rude.'

And she lifted the little mouse out of her pocket, put him down on the ground and walked off.

Tony was feeling as grumpy as a camel. He had the hump, but he still followed Pippin because he didn't know quite what else to do.

And so the two crosspatches tramped along, thinking cross thoughts and forgetting they were supposed to be saving the forest from drying up . . .

UNTIL! Pippin spotted something up ahead, as weird as a beard. She couldn't believe her eyes: it was an enormous EMPEROR PENGUIN. Now, I already know all about this penguin because I am the writer of this book. His name was Count Visbek. He was a big, barrel-shaped brute of a creature. Pippin had to pinch herself to make sure that she was not dreaming. She felt certain that this creature *had to be Shiny* and that it was possible that he might even know why the forest was broken. At the very least, he might be able to help with directions, she thought.

Now, talking to strangers is not a good idea. You know this and I know this and Tony knew this. As it turned out, it was REALLY not a good idea for Pippin to talk to this penguin. It was, in fact, a terribubbly bad idea, because this feathery fellow was a wrong plopper – a very bad wrong plopper indeed. When little Pippin got closer, she could tell just by looking at him that he was a bad news story waiting to happen.

To give you an idea of just how terrible he was, I have asked my friend Rebecca Wiggley to draw him for you on the next page. I want you to close your eyes, turn the page and then open your eyes again

VERY QUICKLY.

Off you go.

'Panicking pancakes!' I hear you freak and you'd be right. I wouldn't like to meet him down a dark alley.

Count Visbek was as mean as he looked (possibly *even meaner*) and, what's worse, he was about to do something so bad to our lovely hero that I am going to have to give it a whole new chapter. That is how bad it is and I am sozzikins to have to make you read it.

Very

sozzikins

indeed.

A Nice
Relaxing Poem

I couldn't bear to write about the bad thing right now because I am a little bit frightened and so I have written a nice relaxing poem instead to help everybody feel nice. It is called 'Birds'.

Birds

Went for a walk
saw a hawk
shouted 'PORK'
made it squawk.

Saw a crow
flying low
where did it go?
I don't know.

by Harry Heape

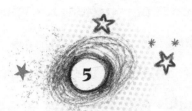

Evil Count Visbek
Does a Very
Bad Thing

Okay friends, my bravery has come back (sozzikins again) and I feel able to continue with the story ...

*

As Pippin approached the penguin, the bad feeling in Tony's tummy got worse and he scampered at a hundred and ten mouse-miles per hour and caught up with his beloved friend. In a flash, he'd sneaked up her trouser leg and back into her shirt pocket.

'Hello, excuse me please, can you help me find the Old Laboratory?' Pippin asked. As the penguin fixed her with his beady eyes, she began to wish that she'd kept her distance. For as well as being mean and scary, this creature didn't smell so good. He glared at the little girl and wheezed and he made the forest smell as though someone had taken the lid off an enormous jam jar full of fish fart.

Count Visbek wore around his neck a lanyard, which read:

Count Visbek
Head of Security
Dr Blowfart's Evil
Scientific Laboratory

Tony buried himself deep into Pippin's shirt pocket. Oh dear, he thought to himself, this must be the Blowfart from my Shine. The one with the horrid cat. The one who likes to do things that are deliciously mean and frightfully rotten. Pippin clutched the little mouse to her heart. They Shined to each other:

I am worried about this petrifying penguin. I want to go home, Shined Pippin.

I know – me too, Tony silently replied.

Let's get out of here, they both Shined – but too late.

Count Visbek cornered Pippin like a schoolyard bully. He began to speak. Now because, so far, Pippin could only Shine with Tony, she did not understand a word of it but I am able to translate for you because I am the boss of this book. The penguin's voice was soft and menacing and his breath smelled like an octopus that had swallowed a load of sea water and was burping it out all over the place. 'What does a horrid little brat like you want to know about an old lab?'

Pippin gulped and the enormous penguin continued, 'You weren't thinking about going up there and snooping around, were you?'

By now, Pippin was scared and she

turned to leave but the enormous fish monster of ocean stink blocked her way. 'Not so fast, little girl!' he wheezed.

Tony had to do something and he had to do it N.O.W. now. He darted out of Pippin's pocket and ran onto her shoulder. Then he jumped onto the wing of the enormous penguin – and bit it so hard that he hit bone.

Visbek's painful squawk echoed loudly around the trees. He stepped backwards and Pippin saw her chance to flee.

'Run, Tony, run!' Pippin screamed.

She ran. Tony ran too. He ran and he *ran*. Tony's little legs felt so fast, it was like he was running on air. In fact, heck-a-doodle-doo!

He WAS running on air – the terrifying penguin had the little mouse's tail in his beak.

'Pippin, help!' pleaded Tony.

Pippin skidded to a halt, turned round and screamed when she saw Tony. **'TONY!** You let him go now or you're going to be in big trouble!' she shouted at Visbek.

The huge penguin laughed and laughed and as he laughed the whole forest became super-smelly with ocean fart. 'You want your little rat, you come and get him!' he wheezed, as he waddled off. To Pippin, the penguin's words just seemed like squawks and shrill screeches. She had a strong feeling that the big mean creature was headed to the Evil Scientific Laboratory. She would follow at a safe distance.

Tony Shined to Pippin, telling her to stay EXACTLY where she was. Pippin replied, telling him that everything would be okay, that somehow she would get help.

She watched as Count Visbek put Tony into a little bag and waddled away into the woods.

Pippin was shell-shocked. But after much sobbing, pacing and I-don't-know-what-to-doing, she had an idea. She looked through Granny's backpack and called up the little old lady on the walkie-talkie.

Granny spoke calmly but very seriously.
'Pippin, my little mushroom, you are both
in great, great danger. A very long time
ago, someone in my family lost their special
Shiny friend ...' Granny's voice began to
tail off – she was obviously upset. 'Pippin ...
he NEVER RECOVERED. You must
rescue Tony without delay. I will help you.
Now, go follow them. I bet my best knickers
this has something to do with the forest
being broken. Run – QUICKLY. I'll join
you as soon as I can.'

Pippin didn't need to be told twice. She leaped up, pocketed the walkie-talkie and slung the backpack over her shoulder. Strange thoughts began racing through her head. Who had this mysterious family member of Granny's been and what exactly had happened to them? But there was no time to waste on thinking – Tony needed rescuing. She began to run like she'd never run before.

Oddplop

Pippin had forgotten all about bringing back the water and trying to fix the broken forest. Now she had a much more important mission: to get inside the Old Laboratory as quickly as possible and rescue her beloved Tony. As soon as she found him she would take him

straight home and shut the door for ever –
maybe longer.

Pippin spotted a sign in the woods
that read:

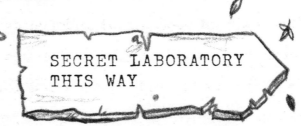

SECRET LABORATORY
THIS WAY

and she ran. She was faster than a rocket-
powered racehorse and arrived just in
time to see Visbek taking Tony inside.
The frightened little mouse felt Pippin
Shine, *I'm coming, Tony. I'm here and
I love you.*

Be very careful, he replied. *I couldn't bear*

it if anything happened to you.

The heavy door shut and the Shine broke. The magic of Shining was ancient and it was fragile, like the elastic on Granny's oldest pair of antique thunderpants – sometimes it worked and sometimes it didn't. Or it could just have been that Tony was too frightened to concentrate – poor little muffin.

Pippin walked around the wrecked Old Laboratory to see if there was another way in. She walked round and around, but the place was like a fart. Gaah, sorry, I am getting nervous as I type – I mean the place was like a FORT!

73

'Sticklebricks!' she harrumphed. 'How AM I going to sneak in?' Pippin needed to work out what to do. She wandered back into the forest, sat up against a tree and looked in the backpack Granny had given her, to see if there was anything she could use to get inside.

Suddenly, something happened that felt stranger than a sunny bank holiday. Our little hero thought she could hear the sound of running water – a sound that hadn't been heard in the forest for a long time. Feeling all of a sudden like a very thirsty Kirsty, she stood up and went to investigate.

Not far at all from the lab, she came

across a small clearing and in the clearing stood a little pool. It was Oswald's Well – a spot the deer visited because it was the only place they could get anything to drink. Pippin was so happy to see the water, she splashed her hot and bothered face and drank deeply. One hundred gulp-a-doodle-doos. Next she ate her hard-boiled eggy-weg, to give her some eggy energy. Then she pulled out her favourite golden powerball from her backpack and started to throw it up and down, catching it each time. This helped her to think.

She threw it up and caught it, higher and higher each time. Then, all of a sudden – big problem – the ball hit a tree and bounced twice, BOING BOING, off two branches before disappearing into the middle of the pool.

'Dagger!' said Pippin. 'That was my best bouncer – I'll never get it back!'

Just as she was not-quite-swearing to herself, Pippin suddenly saw that a very royal-looking frog was watching her. The tiny green creature wore a little bow tie and was cuter than a hundred baby hedgehogs all wearing tiny bandanas. The frog reclined, legs crossed, coolly tapping a tiny foot, as though listening to jazz music. You have just GOT to be able to talk, Pippin thought,

so: 'Hello, what's your name?' she asked.

Now, my lovelies, what Pippin didn't know yet was that not *all* of the animals in the woods were Shiny and able to talk to her. It depended on whether anyone in their family had been touched by the magic stardust long ago. If they had, the gift would have been passed down the generators – oh dear, OOOPSIES! Sorry AGAIN, my friends! I'm still very nervous. I do of course mean *passed down the GENERATIONS!*

But Pippin had the strongest feeling that this little frog *could* understand her, even though she wasn't speaking Croak, the international language of frogs.

The frog stood up and dived gracefully into the pool. There was hardly any splash at all, just a funny little plopping sound and Pippin giggled. It sounded just like when her granny used the bathroom but forgot to close the door.

The frog disappeared for a second or two, then popped up, climbed out right next to Pippin and handed back the powerball. Pippin was gobsmacked. 'Wow! Thanks, whatever-you're-called!'

The frog just looked back at her.

'I know what I'm going to call you,' Pippin said. 'You shall be called Oddplop the Frog Prince – or Oddplop for short.'

Now, Oddplop was one hundred per cent going to talk to her. She knew it. The frog was wearing a bow tie, for goodness' sake!

Pippin waited for the words she felt sure were about to come ... but the two of them just stared at each other. Eventually

Pippin broke the silence. 'Well, I like you, little Oddplop and if it was a normal day I would stay and play. But I really need to get inside the lab – I have a very special mouse to rescue.'

Oddplop smiled, held out a little froggy hand and nodded at the ball. Pippin handed it over and looked into Oddplop's curious beady eyes. Oddplop winked, then hurled the ball out of the clearing, towards the Old Laboratory.

Well, that's frustrating, thought Pippin. 'If you think I'm going to play a game of fetch you've got another think coming.'

As she walked off to collect her ball, she

kept an eye on the frog. Oddplop turned around, did a little pirouette and dived into the pool again.

'Dagger and sticks!' exclaimed Pippin, really annoyed now. 'Oddplop, don't leave me!'

She ran into the grass and spotted her golden powerball over by the Old Laboratory. As she went to pick it up, she looked at the window of the lab and got the fright of her life. There, standing INSIDE the lab and with a big grin on his face, was – guess who? You've got it in one: Oddplop! Pippin nearly fell over. The cute little frog bowed and pretended to fall off the windowsill. Pippin laughed.

Oddplop then disappeared into the room. Pippin twigged what was happening. She raced back to the pool and, sure enough, only a few seconds later the tiny green creature reappeared.

'You clever frog, I knew it! You *can* understand me, can't you? Talk to me then! Talk to me.'

Oddplop opened his mouth and croaked ... 'Rrribbit.'

'Well, that's a start!' smiled Pippin, feeling a tiny bit more magical and Shiny. She got her handy backpack, full of stuff for her mission, changed into the pair of shorts and pulled out her swimming gogglers. Then she stuffed the backpack into the big black bin liner and tied a knot.

Climbing into the pool, Pippin looked at Oddplop, who nodded encouragingly. They both swam into the middle and dived down into the depths of the icy water, Pippin pulling the bin liner behind her.

It was like another world – like the wonderful watery worlds you see on TV shows about wonderful watery worlds. Tiny silver fish swam in shoals and stared as the unlikely pair kicked down towards a small dark cave. Pippin was running out of breath, but as they swam through the cave

the water became shallower and soon she was scrambling onto a stony beach. At the end of the beach was a little metal staircase with a door at the top. Above the door was a sign that said:

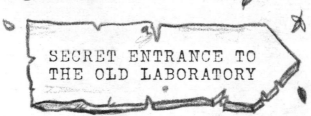

SECRET ENTRANCE TO
THE OLD LABORATORY

The little girl lifted up the cute green frog. 'I'm going to give you a kiss for being so super,' she said, and that's exactly what Pippin did. But Oddplop didn't turn into a prince – because this is not that sort of story, thank heavens.

The Dungeons

It felt cold and creepy inside the lab. All the hairs on the back of Pippin's neck stood up as if they were trying to escape and run home. Pippin knew rescuing Tony would be tricky. The building was huge – it would be like trying to find a noodle in a haystack.

Pippin tried to Shine to Tony to see if she could feel where he was, but she was out of luck. Thinking this was exactly the right time for a cat burglar costume, she quickly changed into the one her granny had given her. As she did, her eye was drawn to a map of the building on the wall. One word in particular leaped out at her:

DUNGEON

Whoever had put up this map (and all those signs!) was obviously a jolly helpful sort of person and if I ever find out who it was, readers, I shall build them a great big cheese and chutney sandwich by way of a thank you.

'That *has* to be where Tony is!' Pippin cried out. 'After all, he's been captured and taken prisoner.'

Oddplop raised an eyebrow and coolly nodded in agreement.

They set off to find the dungeon. At every door they reached, Pippin would stay hidden while Oddplop would peer around the doorway like a frog-shaped periscope on top of her head. This sneaky door move was a clever trick that Pippin had perfected at home with Tony, while playing awesome games like 'Mission Improbable',

'Urgent Speed Crisps' and 'Hungry Ninjas'.
Working together with someone again
felt good, but it made Pippin miss Tony
even more.

Quickly and quietly, Oddplop and Pippin
headed deeper into the depths of the
enormous building. Soon, they came across
a door with a sign taped on it:

MINERS' QUARTERS

And inside, they found something quite
shocking. Now, if you are a nervous sort of
person and you really like animals, it might
be wise to close this book, lock it away and

instead imagine a friendly guinea pig in a little polo shirt gently feeding popcorn to a baby hamster. But if you are curious and inquisitive and very, very brave, then read on ...

What Pippin and Oddplop found was rows upon rows of cages – hundreds of cages – all of them with animals inside. There were SO MANY: badgers, rabbits, voles, rats, more rabbits, hares, shrews, foxes and stoats.

Pippin glanced back towards the sign on the door. If these animals were being kept as slave miners, what were they mining for?

As Pippin and Oddplop wandered

through the darkened room, all the animals put their paws up against the bars. With big wide eyes, they looked at the little girl with the frog on her head. They squeaked and called and grunted and cried and mewed. And they were all saying the same thing:

'*Please help us. Please help us. Please help us.*'

Pippin couldn't understand them, but she saw they were very frightened. She felt so sad and angry. She ran the length of the room, unlocking all the cages. Then she shouted urgently, 'Come quickly! I'll help you to get outside!' But the animals didn't move. In fact, they all seemed to be trying to tell her something. She turned around quickly and—

Smack-whack-crack-thwack!

She clattered right into ... evil Count Visbek.

The enormous emperor penguin looked at Pippin and grinned a big, mean fishy grin.

Quick as a flash, Oddplop jumped off Pippin's head and hid.

Now, my friends, *please* don't think that Oddplop is a cowardy-cowardy custard, don't forget the mustard. Just you wait until you see what this little green marvel had planned! It will blow your hats clean off.

Coming face to face with the monster who'd taken Tony away from her had filled Pippin full of rage. The love she felt for her little mouse was so strong, it made her as brave as nine lions + four tigers + one snake.

'Where's my mouse?' she bellowed. 'Give him back. You can't just take things that don't belong to you!'

The vile penguin leaned into Pippin and prodded the little girl in the chest with his sharp beak. Pippin turned away and Count Visbek began to squawk and push her along the corridor, around the corner and down some stone steps towards the dungeon. Our hero looked around in the gloom. There was junk everywhere – old bits of machinery, tools and several large barrels stacked up in one corner.

Next to the dungeon Pippin saw an enclosure – the kind that you might see at a zoo. And what she saw inside made her heart beat like a big bass drum.

Behind thick metal bars, a smooth concrete wall sloped down steeply, so that whatever was down there had no chance of climbing out. In the pit were shrubs and lots of bones on a dirty muddy floor. Half of the space was taken up with a big pool and submerged in the water was a monstrously massive, muddy-brown crocodile. Pippin could just see a small part of his huge head, half under the water, keeping perfectly still.

'Hello, Tick Tock!' the enormous penguin sneered, looking down at the prehistoric beast.

Pippin, frozen with fear, was transfixed by the sight of the mammoth crocodile. Count Visbek hopped through the bars up onto the ledge of the enclosure. He slid down the concrete slope and into Tick Tock's home. The big fearless penguin waddled around the edges of the cell and lifted some keys off a peg that was located on the far side of Tick

Tock's bed, next to his bedside table and alarm clock. Returning to where he'd left Pippin, the penguin unlocked the dungeon door and threw her inside. Squawking and screeching as he went, Visbek returned the keys to the peg in the crocodile enclosure and waddled off to find Dr Blowfart.

Pippin sank to her knees. She tried Shining to Tony, but could tell immediately that he was *not* in the dungeon, which meant the mission to rescue him had failed miserably.

It was dark in the dank dungeon and it stank of despair. A light had gone out in Pippin's heart and she didn't feel the least bit Shiny. She would not be going home any time soon and there certainly would not be Monster Munch for tea – at least, not the sort of Monster Munch that she'd been hoping for.

The Smell of the
Soft Summer Air

In another part of the forest, Martin the stag, son of King Oswald, was galloping. He had urgency in his eyes and vapour billowing out of both of his nostrilly conk-holes. Every now and then he would stop to check out an interesting sniff-smell or to examine something more closely, searching for any sort of clue that would help solve the mystery of the broken forest.

Martin tried summoning a deeper power. He'd heard his father talk about an ancient magic which had helped him during his many battles, long, long ago. We know what this is, don't we, my fabulous friends. It's Shining! But Martin didn't know that yet. He tried hard to summon some of that magic to help him now. Ooo! He felt a tingling in his nostrils ... but then he sneezed. SLIMPORTANT INFORMATION: It is crucial, my lovely readers, to *always* close your eyes when you sneeze. If you don't, it is possible you will fire your eyeballs huge distances. Always remember this.

Martin searched on the tops of hills and in shady glens and dingly dells. Because Martin wanted to be thorough and check EVERYWHERE, he made sure he also looked in all the dells that weren't dingly and also all the glens that weren't shady.

Soon Martin was back close to where he had started, near Oswald's Well. He then made a full circle around the laboratory, sniffing at the brickwork and looking in through the windows. For a moment, Martin thought he could hear faint mews and cries. He strained to hear properly, but the sound was gone.

He could *smell* something, though. It smelled bitter, muddy and hopeless with a hint of acorns and it was mixed with the smell of fish – smelly fish! – a foul, acrid, nose-curling stink, which made his tummy feel icky.

The young stag's heart was beating fast. This was not a place for animals. It felt unknown and it felt frightening.

Suddenly, a large feathery face appeared at one of the windows. It looked mean and pecky and thoroughly unpleasant. Agh! Martin turned and bolted back into the safety of the trees.

Meanwhile, King Oswald lay snoring on his mossy bed. He was very soundly asleep. In his dreams he was galloping with an old friend. They ran along the banks of the river and they felt powerful and happy. Oswald was never more magical than when he was with this friend – he was bursting with love and joy and it felt exhilarating. He could smell the trees – ash, elder and oak. He could smell and hear animals and birds ... and then it hit him! He knew exactly what was wrong with the forest. He awoke with a start, just as his son arrived, skidding into the clearing and breathing hard.

Urgency coursed through the ancient warrior. 'How did you do, son? What news?'

Martin told his dad of the woods and the strange, unhappy smell at the Old Laboratory.

The king listened intently. 'You have done fantastic work, son – what you have discovered matches something that just came to me while I was sleeping. There were smells on the breeze in my dream, smells that seem so much fainter now. The scents of the foxes, the badgers and the moles ... Why are they not as strong on the breeze as they once were?'

'You're right, Papa! I can't believe we

hadn't noticed,' said Martin. 'Hang on a wink . . . when I was at the Old Laboratory, I thought I could hear mewing and crying too . . .'

The two stags looked in the direction of the ruined laboratory. They could just see its burned and twisted roof. They were silent for a few moments until Oswald spoke. 'Animals are being kept in the Old Laboratory. This is frightening, my son. What is going on? Who would want to kidnap animals?'

'I don't know, but whoever it is, we need to put a stop to it.'

Oswald knew it was time to contact an

old friend for help. He needed to tell her immediately that danger was afoot and that he was on his way. 'Son, I am going to have to leave you for a while,' he said. 'I need you to step up and take charge of the herd.'

Martin felt a surge of pride. He would not let his father down.

Then Oswald, king of the forest, began to do something he had not done in many years. Oswald began to Shine.

And in a cottage not far away, a little silver-haired old lady called Margaret felt the Shine arrive.

It felt magical, bright and sparkly and she began to smile.

Mungo

Back at the dungeon, Pippin's eyes were filling up with large, unhappy tears of salty sadness and she sobbed loudly in the dismal doom.

'Hey, hey! Wing-nut, noggin, half-pint. What are you crying about?'

Pippin looked up. Out from the gloom

came a man. He was huge, with a big friendly face. He looked like nice trouble mixed up with cheeky fun, all squeezed into a tall mischievous body. He wore a

head torch, a scruffy safari jacket which had about a million pockets and a big stripy scarf. 'I'm Mungo,' he announced. 'What's your name?'

'My . . . name . . . is . . . Pippin,' replied our hero, between sobs.

'What are you doing squatting in the mud, Pippin? You look like you're trying to lay an egg. Cheer up and lay me an egg.'

A tiny smile began to form around the edges of Pippin's mouth, and the magic inside her stirred. She didn't know what to make of this man. He was clearly nuts + crackers + bananas, but she was glad he was there. Words spilled out as

109

she explained everything: about being at Granny's, and Shining, and the woods, and Count Visbek and Tony and Oddplop, and the crocodile.

When Pippin came to the end of her story she felt a bit better. 'Will you help me escape?' she asked.

Mungo looked at her with sad eyes. 'Escape, from here? That's impossible. I've been trying for months.'

Mungo began to tell Pippin his story. 'I'm a geologist. I'm nuts about rocks. Big rocks, little rocks, fat rocks, rough rocks, smoooooooth rocks.' Then he sang a funny little song.

♫ *Rocks, rocks, everywhere,*
Rocks, what'll I do?
Rocks, rocks, everywhere,
I think I'll get some rocks for you. ♫

Pippin's mouth popped open in amazement as the big man continued. 'I've been working here for years, studying the caves. We were also looking for diamonds, and we found a few little ones, but not many ... I was doing some research the night Dr Blowfart arrived. There had been a terrible storm. A bolt of lightning had started a fire, and someone said that the Doctor appeared out of the flames. Evil scientists never just ring the doorbell or knock politely – have you noticed that?'

Pippin looked wide-eyed at the big funny man and nodded. Mungo continued. 'That night, all my colleagues ran away, but I went back for my wicked rock collection and foolishly got caught. I've been kept prisoner ever since.' He gave a sigh. 'The evil Doctor has been trying to use my specialist geological knowledge to try to predict where the biggest diamonds might be found. And then Blowfart started kidnapping forest creatures to mine for diamonds!' Mungo added, clearly distressed.

'What a monster!' gasped Pippin.

'The Doctor is obsessed with finding one particular diamond,' Mungo explained. 'One he calls "El Más Brillante". He dammed the river to divert the water away from the caves so he could mine right down inside them. He is a clever fellow and he built a huge super-quiet fan to blow away all the rain clouds so the caves couldn't flood again – all this to find a stone! The diamond is supposed to be HUGE though, with amazing powers. Blowfart's loopy about it.'

But Pippin was distracted. She kept hearing little disgusting burps. 'Will you stop that yuckity burpering!' she begged Mungo.

'But that wasn't me,' Mungo protested. 'It's coming from outside!' They both heard the sound again and looked up.

'Rrrrruuubaattt.'

'Wait a minute, that's not burping,' said Mungo ...

'Oddplop!' Pippin squealed in delight.

She and Mungo rushed over to the door and there, standing in between the bars, was Oddplop the Frog Prince.

'Yay! Oddplop, quick! We need you to sneak into that tank and pinch the dungeon keys from the crocodile.'

'That's crazy,' yelled Mungo. 'You can't send that tiny frog in there!'

Oddplop looked at Pippin, winked at the big geologist and sprang silently up onto the wall of Tick Tock's enclosure, where he did a couple of little stretches, like an athlete limbering up.

The little frog and the enormous crocodile began to talk, though Pippin had no idea what they were saying. (You see, Pippin still hadn't properly worked out how to Shine to other animals yet.) To Mungo and Pippin it all just sounded like a load of croaks and hisses. But because I am lovely and funusually kind, I will tell you what they said. Here we go:

'You have something I need, *amigo*,' began Oddplop.

'Oh yesss? And what might that be, sssunshhhine?' asked the crocodile.

'The keys, *amigo*. My friends, they have been wrongly imprisoned and I intend to set-a-them free. So why not flick them over here and then there won't be any trouble,' said Oddplop, reasonably.

'No can do, I'm afffffraid,' hissed the crocodile. 'You'll have to come and get them …' And he opened his mouth just a tiny bit.

Oddplop looked straight at the crocodile's huge, mean, ancient face and spoke calmly.

'When I come inside that tank – me, a tiny little frog – and take the keys from you – a huge and powerful crocodile – you will feel crushed. Your confidence will never recover.'

The crocodile shifted his weight from one side to the other, readying himself. 'The moment you ssset foot inside thisss tank, I will sssnap my jaws around you so fasssst, you will not know whether you are coming or going. And then when you realise that you are mosssst ccccertainly *going*, I will ssswallow you whole and that will be that.'

'Okay,' replied the little frog. 'I did try to

warn you.' And before you could say 'Bob's your uncle', there was a blur of green.

The crocodile looked at Oddplop. 'Well,' he hissed, 'I'm ready when you are.'

Oddplop held up the dungeon keys and jangled them at Tick Tock. 'I've already been in and out, *amigo* – that green flash was me. I went in off your crusty beak, nabbed the keys and was back before you could say "oh dear". I even had time to nip into your bed and fart under the duvet.'

The crocodile was livid. He started thwacking his tail around. 'Get back in here – I'll tear you to piecesss!'

The frog smiled and said quietly, 'You

will do nothing of the sort, because I am too cool for school and you, my friend, are all mouth and no trousers.' And with that, the little frog jumped off the wall and delivered the keys to Pippin and Mungo.

How cool is that, everybody?

In an instant, Pippin and Mungo were out. 'You are the most fantastic frog in the whole pondiverse,' beamed Pippin, placing her little froggy friend back on top of her head, where Oddplop sat very happily indeed.

Everything felt good and the idea of rescuing Tony and mending the broken forest felt very possible indeed, but then something

ENORMOUSLY **BAD** happened. The gang heard voices and just managed to duck out of sight behind a stack of barrels. Dr Blowfart swept in, like a mad professor. He was tall and spindly, with swept-back grey hair. He wore a white lab coat and he looked like he hadn't eaten in years. The doctor was followed by his horrid fluffy cat, Gareth, and Count Visbek, who immediately saw that the door to the dungeon was open.

Pippin could not understand what the mean emperor penguin was saying but I can tell you that he was frightened. 'I don't understand,' he squawked to his master. 'The girl was locked in there! This is impossible.'

Finally, after several moments of icy silence, Blowfart looked at Visbek and spoke menacingly. 'You let me down once in the forest when you only managed to capture her mouse. You have let me down again – she has escaped, AGAIN. COME HERE, YOU MISERABLE FOOL!'

Blowfart stood in front of Visbek and bellowed a cyclone of fury at him. It looked as though the huge penguin was being blasted by a jet engine: as the Doctor roared, the penguin's feathers blew backwards. 'Find the girl! IMMEDIATELY, or I shall feed YOU to my crocodile!' he screeched.

The Doctor walked over to the open

dungeon door and examined the room. He turned back and looked around very carefully. His eyes seemed to linger on the barrels. *The barrels where Pippin and Mungo and Oddplop were hiding!*

Will Blowfart find our heroes and lock them up for ever, or will they *somehow* manage to escape?

I am afraid that I cannot tell you right now, because tonight is my bath night and I need to go and wash my wig and my alarmpits, charmpits, farmpits. You will all have to wait until tomorrow to find out. Sozzers.

Big Proglems

Deer Readerers,

I cannot write anything toady because there is a big proglems with my somputer keybeard.

I am vory serry, especially after the fonsense about washnig my alarmpits. I know that we are at a nimportant fart of the story. I will need to wisit Ye Olde PC Worlde Shop and get the keybeard monded immediaterly. Will write more tomorrabs. Promproms.

Fandest regords,

Hairy Heape

Authorer

A Really Bad
Thing Happens

Computer mended! Yay. Thank you for your patience. Where were we? Oh yes – our friends were hiding behind the barrels by the dungeon. Remember? Not really?

Here's a little reminderoony.

The Doctor walked over to the open dungeon door and examined the room. He turned back and looked around very carefully. His eyes seemed to linger on the barrels.

Now this is when the **really bad thing** happens. The **really bad thing** that is in the title of this chapter. If you don't like reading about **really bad things** then I would go and eat some honey on toast or something like that, because right now, a **really bad thing** is definitely about to happen . . .

Tony suddenly appeared out of the Doctor's jacket pocket. *Tony!* Shined Pippin. *I'm here and I love you.*

But then (oh dear, my lovely readers, I can't bear to tell you ...)

Maybe I won't tell you.

OK, maybe I will.

Maybe I won't.

No, I will.

Argh. No, I can't.

But I must.

Okay. Here goes ...

Tony scurried up and whispered into Blowfart's ear: 'Sir, the little girl is hiding behind the barrels.'

Do you see what I mean? Do you see why I didn't want to tell you? Tony the mouse had betrayed his bestest friend in the world, Pippin.

The Doctor laughed long and hard. 'Hahahahahahaha hahahahahaha.

'HOW fantastic!'

Even though Tony had whispered, Pippin had heard him because of her Shiny powers and now our little hero felt completely crushed.

She'd been betrayed by her best best best friend in the world. It was as though a light had been switched off in her heart. Her whole body went weak and she collapsed like a rag doll.

'Seize them, you fool,' Blowfart spat in the direction of Count Visbek, pointing at the barrels behind which our heroes were hiding.

'Oh no you don't!' Mungo swung one

of his huge arms and the barrels clattered over in the direction of our terrible baddies. The villains scattered like skittles as Mungo scooped up dear Pippin and Oddplop and ran for the exit, sprinting as if he was possessed by Quickos, the Greek god of speed. He flew up the stairs three at a time and was out of sight in a third of a moment, or *mo* for short.

'After them, you IDIOT!!' roared Blowfart to Count Visbek (who was just picking himself up off the floor). Scarified of what the Doctor might do to him if he let Pippin escape AGAIN AGAIN, the penguin waddle-dashed up the stairs

132

in pecky pursuit.

Halfway up the stairs, little Oddplop made a split-second decision to remain in the lab. The clever little frog sprang onto the top of a door frame and crouched down low, like a total boss.

Now I know what you are thinkering – ANOTHER yellow-bellied cowardy custard manoeuvre from little Oddplop. But what did I tell you last time? That's right – just wait and see!

With Pippin over one shoulder, the crazy geologist Mungo hurtled through corridors, in and out of rooms and up staircases as he tried to escape. Worryingly he was now growing tired and no longer felt possessed by Quickos. Visbek was gaining on him, so the big geologist slammed doors, pulled bookcases over and ripped shelves off the wall to block the enormous penguin. Mungo knew the Old Laboratory well and like a roller-skating rhino he took the quickest route out into the safety of the forest.

Visbek darted off to a supply room, just as Mungo smashed through the Old Laboratory's main doors and into the sunshine. The lovely big fool was going as fast as he could, sprinting into the forest like a man being chased by a thousand angry toilets.

Visbek reappeared moments later with an enormous net and stood staring into the forest. He heard rustling and saw branches moving in the distance. His eyes narrowed and he sniffed at the air and then, like a feathery pecky tank, he trundled off into the woods.

The Number One
Golden Rule
of Shining

Back at the Old Laboratory, Tony was in a cage on Dr Blowfart's desk, which was cluttered with reams of mad scribbley-papers, test tubes and a pair of science goggles. The little mouse was feeling very, very sad and had decided that he was going to stay in the little toilet roll that was now his bed forever. Forever and **ever** and **ever** and **ever** or maybe even

LONGER.

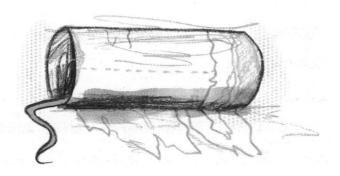

Tony asked himself the same question over and over: why had he given his best friend away? Then he heard a voice.

'Pssst! Hey, *amigo*. I need to talk to you.'

Tony opened his eyes and peeped out of the end of the toilet roll.

'Pssst! Hey, *amigo*. *AMIGO*, HEY! Get your mousey booty out here – there is not much time.'

Why was a little green frog in a bow tie trying to get traitorous Tony to come out of his hiding place?

'I'm never coming out,' groaned Tony.

'Listen to me. If you want to save Pippin, then you need to come out right away

and make some very important-quick-fast-
chatty-time with me now.'

Tony crawled out of his tube. 'I
can't possibly save her,' he cried. 'I
betrayed her!'

Oddplop was hopping about like there
was no time to lose.

'Listen, my little mousey friend. We
CAN save her and you better believe it.
But you have to listen to me very carefully
and do exactly as I tell you. Your Pippin is
Shiny. Yes?'

Tony nodded.

Oddplop continued: 'The evil Doctor –
he is Shiny too, but his gift is VERY

STRONG. So, Pippin's Shining is like the Babybel and his Shining is like the huge smelly ten kilos of Stilton. Yes?'

Tony nodded. This frog was talking his language.

'That is because of the Number One Golden Rule of Shining!' explained the little frog. 'You need to trust each other to make new friends. It needs to be okay for her to talk to other animals – tell her. That's how Shining works, how it blooms and how it grows. You and Pippin need each other, of course you do, but you also need other people. We all do.'

The funny little frog was starting to make sense and Tony began to feel a bit more ploptimistic.

'She trusts you to talk to others. Yes?'
Oddplop asked.

Tony thought back to that morning in
Granny's cellar, when Pippin had said it was
okay for the little mouse to talk to humans.
He remembered her words perfectly ...

*I would love it if Tony could talk to other
people too – I'm sure he'd like that.*

But then Tony had said:

I don't want you to talk to anyone else.

Tony looked at the frog. 'She trusted me.
But I didn't trust her back and now she's in
danger and it's all my fault!'

'It's not your fault – it's the fault of the

Doctor. He was able to control your mind. It wasn't you that gave away where Pippin was hiding – it was a Shiny mind trick!'

Tony looked at Oddplop. He hadn't understood how he could have done anything so awful but now it was making more sense.

'It was most certainly not your fault, *amigo*, but you CAN still put this right. Shine to Pippin. Tell her that she can talk with other animals. It will make her instantly a million times more powerful. She is being chased, but if you let her, she can ask the forest animals for help.'

Tony held onto the bars of his cage and

tried with every muscle in his tiny body to get a Shine through. He tried and he tried. Nothing happened except that he did an unhappy little poop. He tried again and again. Still nothing.

'You gotta keep going, *amigo*. Keep trying!'

So Tony did try; he tried with all his might. And then – wondrous, wonderful wonders!! – a Shine began to grow ...

A Brand New Feeling

Out in the sunshine, Pippin was feeling very bad. She was still being carried by Mungo, the lovely big geologist, which was a bit like being thrashed around in a washing machine, but that wasn't what was making her feel so sick. She was being hunted by a big pecky penguin with an enormous net, but that wasn't what was making her feel so desperate. The evil Doctor and his mean fluffy white cat were busy being beastly, but THAT wasn't what was making her feel so incredibubbly sad-bad either.

What had emptied her heart of joy was the fact that her best friend in the world had turned against her.

But as they ran, she thought about it. And the more she thought about it, the more ridiculous it seemed. Tony would never do that. He'd just NEVER do that, she repeated to herself. Tony would never do that. He'd never do that.

Ever.

    Ever.

        Never.

            Ever.   Ever.

Suddenly a smile crept across Pippin's face. Ancient Shiny magic from all around the galaxy began to course through her and she felt a brilliant brightness inside her tummy. She recognised the feeling and she grinned. It was the start of a Shine!

Pippin, it's me. It's Tony. I am SO sorry. But it wasn't my fault. It was that horrible, horrible Doctor. He turned my mind to jelly to find you and controlled my voice. I would NEVER betray you.

I know you wouldn't, replied Pippin. *I was just saying exactly the same thing to myself. But don't worry, Tony. I'm coming back for you. I promise.*

And I can help you, Pippin! There's something I have to tell you, Tony Shined. *It's my fault that you can't Shine with other animals yet. That funny frog just filled me in on the Number One Golden Rule of Shining: I have to trust you – and I do! You should have as many friends as you want, not just me. I was being shelfish and shilly. The more friends, the better. In fact, someone right here would like a word with you.*

Then, something new and marvellously

147

and magnificently magical happened to
Pippin – for the first time, she began to
Shine with ANOTHER ANIMAL.

Hello, amiga, Shined the little frog Oddplop.

Oddplop, is that you? asked Pippin, tears of super-excited joy streaming down her face, utterly beside herself with magical, twinkly, happy-wappy weepiness.

Yes. It is me. I am the frog that you call Oddplop. But my real name is not Oddplop. My name is Maria.

Maria! Shined Pippin. *You are a GIRL FROG!*

Yes, I am. You can still call me Oddplop because I quite like it, amiga. But I am most certainly not a frog prince.

Okay! Pippin replied. *I want to cuddle you, Maria the Frog Princess! Thanks for everything you have done for me – you have been a million times awesome!*

Back in the Old Laboratory, Oddplop just blew at her imaginary froggy fingernails and let out a cute little soft whistle, looking bashful. *My pleasure, amiga,* she coolly Shined. *Now. You need to call out to the forest creatures to help you and for sure they will come. Tony and I will go now and we will keep safe.*

Okay, Shined Pippin.

Love you, Shined Tony.

Love you too, Pippin Shined back.

The Shine fizzed, twinkled and then, like a happy bubble, it popped and was gone.

Feeling ninety-thousand per cent happy and fifty-thousand per cent nice, Pippin wasted no time and began the most important, Shiniest Shine of her whole life.

Animals of the forest, I need your help! Please come. We need to get away from a beastly penguin who is chasing us, so that we can rescue lots of animals that are being kept prisoner by an evil doctor. Please come and help, please!

She Shined it again and again and again under the sun-speckled canopy of the beautiful trees, listening to Mungo bellow like a warthog as he ran.

And, lo! In a distant corner of the forest,

Martin the young stag looked up. FOR THE FIRST TIME IN HIS LIFE HE WAS FEELING A SHINE TOO! He seemed to grow in size as the magic coursed through his body. He saw birds taking off and all flying in the same direction. He saw woodland animals coming out of their burrows. All around, the forest was stirring and all its Shiny animals were coming to find this little girl who so desperately needed their help. Martin began to gallop at an incredible speed towards the feel of the Shine.

When, poor pooped-out Mungo could run no more, he collapsed in a clearing, boo – just as all the animals began to arrive, hooray! BUT – OH NO – a hundred-and-ten boos with an enormous side order of double-boo, beastly Visbek arrived too. He crept up on poor Pippin and Mungo. The big mean penguin had them cornered and he began to raise his enormous fishing net, swinging it like a lasso around his feathery head, waiting to release it and trap his prey.

But don't worry, little friends. What happened next was funexpected, funcredibubble and funbelievable!

Martin the stag arrived like a majestic steam train, crashing through the trees and into the clearing. Hooves clattered, dust flew and the noise was deafening.

In a lickety-split second, Martin whipped the net from Count Visbek and scooped him up with it. Martin was feeling so Shiny and powerful that he flung the net up into a tree, where it caught on a branch. The flapping emperor penguin was snagged and bagged like an angry turkey. HOORAY and BOOYAKA!!!

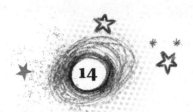

Beloved Friends

Now, my nice readerers. Have you been wondering what on *oeuf* has been going down with Granny and Oswald? I have, but I'll keep this bit of the story as small as the wrist of a tiny little vole, because, as you know, important ACTION is happening in the forest.

The last we heard was that the king of the forest had sent a Shine to a lady called Margaret. Can you remember who that is? Bang on! You do have a good memory – it was Granny's real lady human name. This was Granny and Oswald's first Shine in many, many years.

The Shine contained feelings of warmth and love and Oswald told Granny of the forest and the water and the missing animals. Granny told Oswald of Pippin and Tony. Then there was a pause until they both Shined exactly the same thing to each other: *THE DOCTOR. I THINK HE'S BACK!*

Granny and Oswald had a long history with Blowfart. They'd had a great many run-ins back when they were all young. Granny had battled with him on top of a fast-moving train. She'd fought a duel with him on a rickety old rope bridge over the Zambezi River. She had thought that she'd caught him, only to see him escape at the last moment like a burp at a barbecue.

And Granny had always tried to talk Blowfart into changing his ways. She had known him before the darkness had enveloped his life and she wanted desperately to help him to recover and be happy once more.

King Oswald the stag, however, was much less forgiving. Many of his scars had come from fierce battles with the evil Doctor and the warrior in him felt that Blowfart was too far gone to be saved.

Our two old friends finished their warm and loving Shine. They both knew there wasn't a moment to lose. It was time to drag their old bones into ACTION!

Turbo

Back in the forest, Pippin had changed out of her cat burglar costume because it felt itchy, titchy and a little bit bumcomfortable. Now she was sitting with Mungo and their new woodland friends. Martin approached them, still breathless from his exceedingly daring rescue.

'Thank you!' Pippin smiled at the brave young stag.

Martin beamed. He felt incredible because HE COULD UNDERSTAND PIPPIN. He could Shine with her!

'You're welcome,' he said to the little girl. 'My name's Martin,' he added proudly, and the little girl gave his coat a ruffle.

'What happens next?' Pippin wondered aloud.

Although Mungo could not talk to animals, he thanked Martin with a friendly embrace. 'We need to rescue Tony, Oddplop and the other animals,' he began urgently. 'We need to re-flood the mines and we need to do SOMETHING about the Doctor. This has gone far enough.'

Pippin translated for her animal friends – superfast. Because she was good like that.

'I am one of the country's leading geologists!' Mungo continued, with a wink and a raise of his eyebrows. 'I know exactly how to bring back the rain and flood the mines. That'll be as simple as a pimple – I'll just destroy the fan. Then I'll bust up the dam. But if ONLY we had some dynamite – that would make it all so much quicker.'

'I have some of Granny's dynamite in my backpack!' Pippin chimed proudly. This was NOT a sentence she had ever thought she'd be saying. 'But how can we do the rescuing?' she asked.

'We'll break in again,' Mungo replied. 'They won't be expecting us to go *back*. Martin is brilliant at rescuing, as he's just proved – he can free all the mining animals.'

Mungo was thinking. He was a man on a mission. He looked at Pippin. 'The really big difficult thing, the one-millionty-dollar question is: after we rescue everyone, what are we going to do with evil Dr Blowfart?'

Pippin communicated everything to Martin and the other animals, and now the forest fell silent. Just the thought of Blowfart was enough to make everyone freeze in their tracks.

'Pippin,' Mungo began and then he paused, looking intently at the little girl. 'It's going to have to be you who does it – I'll be busy blowing up the DAM a-lam-a-ding-dong.'

Pippin nodded. 'I have had more than enough of the Doctor's mean ways. I want him locked up forever and I will do everything I can to make that happen,' she vowed with steely determination. The animals of the forest began clapping. Even the ones who hadn't a clue what she'd just said.

Mungo smiled at his brave little chum-pal.

'Let's do it!' Pippin yelled. 'With all of us working together, we can accomplish anything,' she added proudly, looking at all her new friends.

'ROCKING!' cried Mungo. 'We got the power! Now what we need are some suggestions about how we're actually going to do it. Let's brainstorm.'

A chubby magpie hopped up next to Pippin. Funnily enough, his name was Chubby. *Everyone* called him Chubby – EVEN HIS MOTHER. 'I'll go,' he chirped. 'I'm not scared. I live my life on the edge, because I'm a cheeky thief from the wrong side of town and I'm not afraid of a bit of dangerous danger; I'm a tasty gangster and I will do *whatever* it takes.'

'Hang on a second!' piped up a hedgehog. 'We all know what you're like, Chubby. You're UNRELIABLE – if you see something shiny, you'll just disappear with it and we won't see you again for an hour.'

'HOW DARE YOU!' replied Chubby indignantly. 'I've never been so insulted in all my— Ooh, look! A milk-bottle top . . .'

And Chubby the magpie hopped under a bush, picked up the shiny milk-bottle top

and flew off, squawking back at them as he went, 'I just need to put this somewhere safe . . . !'

They all tried to think in their woodland think tank. It was tricky. The good ideas cupboard was as empty as a pauper's pocket. One by one their thought bubbles popped into nothingness.

Chubby swooped back down, looking as pleased as punch. 'Right,' he tweeted, 'I've put that lovely milk-bottle top with the rest of my treasure. Now what have I missed? I want you to tell me all about it and don't skip anythi— Ooh, look! Is that some tinsel? I love tinsel. It's my favourite. Oh no, it's just some string. Sorry, I'm a sucker for shiny stuff.'

'Shut up, Chubby!' the animals all shouted angrily.

'Wait! That's it!' cried Pippin. 'That's IT!'

'What's it?' asked Martin, pacing. He was restless and really wanted to get going.

'I've got it! Blowfart is just like Chubby. The Doctor's obsessed with finding the big shiny diamond, El Más Brillante. That's his weakness. If we can trick him into thinking we have the diamond, then maybe ... Oh, I don't know what yet – but I'm sure that's the way to get him. It must be!'

'Maximum plannage!' cried Mungo suddenly. 'I've got it. Listen up, here it is. Pippin, you go into the mines with an animal volunteer. I've got a map to help you navigate the tunnels. Get the little animal to pretend that they're a miner and that they've found the stone!'

'Yes!' beamed Pippin, her eyes dancing with excitement. 'Then what?'

'Blowfart comes down and the pretend miner tells him it's at the back of the cave, still stuck in the rock. Blowfart goes in to see it and then . . .' Mungo picked up a stick of dynamite. 'Ka-boom, rubble trouble! You blow up the entrance to the cave and Blowfart is trapped until we can fetch an army of police people.'

Pippin cracked a very big smile, because she knew that this was a very, very good plan. She jumped up and down on one leg and clapped because she was so hoppy and she gave Mungo a big hug.

Then Pippin's heart sank because she knew there was a very, very big problem. They needed an animal volunteer, someone brave enough to act as the pretend miner to lure Blowfart into their trap. And they needed an animal strong enough to resist the Doctor's mind games: Pippin knew that if the Doctor read this creature's mind and realised that the diamond discovery was a trick, then it could be a hundred-and-twenty

171

bad multiplied by a billion big bads to the power of bad. It could mean certain pain for that little animal.

Question: Who would take on such a job?

Answer: No one in their right mind.

Pippin spoke to the animals and explained about the danger and the mind reading. Everyone was silent and nobody would meet Pippin's gaze.

Then a bouncy little badger stepped out of the crowd. He clasped his tiny paws together and shuffled. He gulped, then before he could stop himself, blurted out:

'Sounds like a job for TURBO – **OH YEAHHHHH!'**

All the animals began to cheer. They mobbed Turbo and they cuddled him and sat on him as if he was a lovely warm duck egg and with that, their brilliant and very planny plan was hatched.

Something Baaaad
about the Plaaaan

It was decided. Pippin would go into the mines with the bouncy little badger. His real name was Alan, but he preferred to call himself Turbo because it was just a tiny bit more glamorous. No offence to any Alans out there.

As you know, my lovely readers, Pippin was a little girl and like most girls her age, she had a very slender amount of experience in handling dangerous explosives.

'I'm not feeling totally comfortable about the dynamite bit of the plan,' she admitted to Mungo. 'Where do I stand? How do I light it? And how long before it goes and does its enormous and very dangerous explodering?'

Mungo had made lots of things explode before because he was a big naughty geologist and he pulled out a piece of dynamite and gave Pippin a quick lesson.

He showed her the fuse, which is the stringy thingy bit at the end and explained that it would be just like lighting a sparkler. Pippin absolutely hated lighting sparklers, but thought it best not to mention this.

'Once it's lit,' continued Mungo, 'you've probably got about fifteen seconds to get out of the cave.' This did not make Pippin feel much better and she wished quite a lot that she could have Mungo the rock-star geologist with her for the exploding bit, but she knew this was not possible.

They would make the first part of the journey all together: Pippin and Turbo, Martin and Mungo and his helpers (for he was to be assisted by Geoff the stoat and Snape the little lamb).

Everyone was feeling positive until Snape piped up. 'There is something baaaad about this plaaan.'

Pippin and Martin stopped and looked down at her. 'What do you mean?' the stag asked.

'Well,' began the lamb, 'if we blow up the daaaam to make the mines flood and you haven't yet sealed in the Doctor, what happens if you get traaaapped by the waaaater?'

'Hmm,' pondered Pippin. 'We have to blow the dam to fix the forest. So Mungo, how long have we got between you blowing up the dam and the mines flooding?'

'Ten minutes,' replied the rockonologist. 'Ten minutes max.'

Pippin looked back at the gang. 'Then it's easy. As soon as Turbo Alan and I hear Mungo's explosion, we know how long we have. If our time is up, we'll just have to run like the wind.'

It was risky. The timings would be crucial. What could go wrong? Everyone knew the answer was 'plenty', but no one was saying it.

Pippin's new woodland friends were anxious to know when they would see her again. Pippin carefully explained that they would also have to wait for the signal. When they heard Mungo blow up the dam with the dynamite, they should head to the agreed meeting place on the craggy cliff top above the mines and the lab. Mungo and Pippin and Turbo and Martin would make their way there too, when each of them had completed their mission.

There was much nodding and mewing and excited animal chatter and then at last they set off. The animals cheered their brave heroes and they all felt like jolly good fellows.

'They'll probably make me mayor after all

this,' grinned Mungo. 'I'll be a hero. Being mayor would be skillage in the village.'

'Er, why?' asked Pippin. She couldn't think of anything worse than being mayor, spending all day shaking hands with babies and patting people on the head. She wondered if Mungo's brain box had finally spring-onioned a leek.

'Er, hello?' said Mungo. 'BIG RED COAT! And all the gangsta chains. I'd be the baddest mayor in England. But better than the coat and the jewels – if you are mayor then you're allowed to take fire engines home at weekends.'

'I'm pretty sure you're not,' Pippin

replied. 'Are you as certain as a curtain?' She grinned.

'Definitely,' Mungo replied. 'Having a weekend fire engine would be maximum sweet.'

The animals – Martin, Turbo, Snape and Geoff – looked at the big foolish fool as he yicketed on endlessly. They had no idea what he was talking about, but they knew it was complete hogscribble and they loved him very much for it.

With all the nice chatting, time passed quickly and soon they were there. They were at the end of the yummiest part of the journey, the part they could make together.

The forest path they had been treading forked – one way climbed up a steep hill that led to the top where the dam and the super-silent fan were; the other way continued into the woods to the lab. And just a few yardsticks away stood the entrance to the caves where their trap would be laid.

After a hug from Pippin and Mungo, Martin made his way down the winding path that led to the lab. Seeing him go made Pippin wibble-wobble.

Mungo looked at Pippin and saw that her face had turned from happy to very sad, so he tried to reassure her. 'The Doctor is bonkers about the diamond and our plan is STRONGER THAN A GIANT'S TROUSERS. All you need to do is light the dynamite and seal him in.'

Mungo pulled out a box of matches and gave the little girl a handful. 'You can strike these on the wall of the cave,' he said. 'I'll take the box.'

Pippin was still frightened and the big guy knew it. He picked her up and hugged her and gave her hair a last ruffle. 'We'll meet up as soon as we've done our jobs. Good luck.'

'Thanks,' Pippin replied. 'You too.' Then she turned on her heel and, together with Turbo Alan, walked into the cave. And though she was scared she didn't look back – not even a little bit – because she knew if she did it would make her feel as wonky as a donkey. And now was not the time for wonkiness, nor was it the time for donkeyness.

A Very
Important Fart

Mungo bounded up the hill like a
man possessed – this time a man
possessed by a bigger, much more
stupid man. He had Snape and Geoff on
his shoulders and even though he knew

they couldn't funderstand him, he talked to them non-stop with cheeky mischief in his naughty eyes.

But as he bounced and chatted, something terribad happened. the box of matches wriggled and jiggled out of his coat pocket and fell onto the floor. Mungo didn't even notice. He was too busy thinking about lovely rocks, fire engines and what it would be like to be mayor.

Finally Mungo reached the huge fan that had been blowing the rain clouds away from Funsprings. It made him feel one-hundred happy and nine-hundred nice because the fan was enormous and he was looking forward to busting it. His idea about how to do this made him so happy he wanted to say 'woo-hoo' out loud.

'Woo-hoo!' he said out loud.

This was his idea:

THROW BIG ENORMOUS ROCKS OF OUCH WHACK.

Mungo ran around gathering a huge pile of stones to hurl. Geoff the stoat saw what he was doing and began to help. They were both very much enjoying their job.

Snape the little lamb was excited too. She couldn't gather rocks because her hooves were rubbish for that sort of thing, so she tried to help by thinking up a song she could sing as encouragement during this important time.

Soon Mungo and Geoff had plenty of

rocks, so Mungo started hurling them hard, trying to hit the big fan right on its hooter.

Unfortunately, his aim was rubbish. For a while he didn't even come close to hitting the fan – which, considering it was as big as a house, gives you a good idea how useless he was at throwing.

Geoff looked at Snape and moaned despairingly, 'This guy's pants. He couldn't hit a cow's bum-bum with a banjo.'

'We have to belieeeve,' baaaed Snape, and she started to sing her song. I want you to sing along at home too. ALL OF YOU, *especially* any grown-ups. I'll sing too – it will help Mungo, I pinkie-promise. Sing!

♫ Hey there, farty farty, ♫
Farting is fun to do.
Hey there, farty farty,
I wanna fart with you.

♫

This song made Snape and Geoff feel better and after the first verse Mungo managed to at least hit the fan, which was definitely progress.

This gave them hope, so Geoff joined in with the second verse, which luckily was just the same as the first, only a little bit *FASTER*. Sing!!

♫ *Hey there, farty farty,* ♫
Farting is fun to do.
Hey there, farty farty,
I wanna fart with you.

♫

The big geologist hit the fan again. He had no idea that the racket behind him was the animals singing, but if he had known, he would have liked the song A GREAT DEAL. And it seemed to be helping, because he was getting closer and closer to his target.

'One more verse should do it,' baaaed Snape, so they sang it a little bit *FASTER* still. SING!!!

♫ Hey there, farty farty, ♫
Farting is fun to do.
Hey there, farty farty,
I wanna fart with you!

♫

Just as Snape the lamb and Geoff the stoat sang the final 'fart', Mungo hit gold. A huge lump of rock torpedoed straight into the middle of the fan's control panel, causing it to explode with a big bang of bad flashy damage sparkles. The fan groaned to a halt.

Mungo jogged around low-fiving the stoat and the little lamb and doing rubbish body-popping.

Now they had to move onto the dam, which luckily was so close by that you could have thrown a stone at it, although if big silly Mungo had tried this it would probably have hit Geoff the stoat on the end of his long stoaty snout-beak instead.

Very quickly, Mungo emptied out his backpack and made a pile of the things that he needed: rope, which he'd borrowed from Pippin; a grappling hook, which he'd made out of Pippin's rubber chicken (do you remember the rubber chicken from the beginning of this adventure? Of course you do, because you have the remembering skills to pay the remembering bills); and finally the two most importconk things: dynamite and matches. He found the dynamite. Matches . . . Where were the matches? He checked all his pockets. Then he checked them again.

'Aaaaarghh!
'No matches!!!!'

Game over, you're thinking, right?
WRONG!

It was okay, because luckily Mungo was Mungo and apart from breaking things and climbing things, his main childhood hobby had been setting fire to things.

Obviously setting fire to things is very dangerous and you should not choose it as a hobby. If you are looking for a hobby, try something cool like street dancing, playing the guitar, or making biscuits for your favourite author.

Now, back to the story! Mungo found his geologist's magnifying glass. 'Aha,' he said, grinning like a maniac. 'This might just save the day.'

Next, he ran around fetching bits of dry moss and tiny twigs and then some bigger twigs. He scrunched the dry moss and twigs into a little ball and positioned himself with his back to the sun. But he didn't have

197

much time. Now that the huge fan had been broken, the first clouds in a year were drifting towards Funsprings.

Quickly, Mungo tilted the magnifying glass so that it caught the sun. A bright little dot appeared on the moss. He focused the light and kept very still. The fire began to smoke but it still wasn't hot enough to catch. 'Big poopy unicorn,' sort-of-swore Mungo.

Then he had an idea. He reached into his back pocket and pulled out a dry and crusty paper hanky. He put this on top of the woody nest. Then he gestured for the little stoat to come and hold the magnifying glass, which Geoff did.

Mungo had one last trick up his sleeve. He bent down over the moss and tried to fart. His face contorted in concentration and he went cross-eyed. 'Come on . . . come to papa,' he begged. 'Time to rock and roll.'

Just a second before the sun disappeared behind a big cloud, Mungo squeezed out one long, very hot, high-pitched, perfectly directed fart. It was enough! There was a huge *woomph* and the hanky caught fire. 'Yay!' Mungo danced. 'Hurray for me and my big and clever farting!'

He lit the fuse at the now roaring fire and ran to the dam, quickly tying the dynamite to the rope on the way. He hopped right onto the top of the dam and moonwalked backwards along it, to the middle, where he lowered the rubber chicken grappling hook with the stick of dynamite tied to it, burning and spitting and sizzling. He lowered it until it sat right in the middle of the dam, resting against the wall and then he ran back as fast as he could. He was just about to reach the bank when—

The dynamite blew up, taking the whole of the middle section of the dam to kingdom come.

And as the dam exploderated, Mungo dived to safety, like a much bigger and much more silly James Bond.

El Más
Brillante

Underground, where everything was cold and smelled of miserable potatoes, Pippin and Turbo had been making slow progress. It was dark, the uneven, slippery floor was hard to walk on and it was really hard to tell if they were going in the right direction. There were no landmarks, no helpful signposts and no police ladies or lolliplop men to help them on their way.

Head torch on, Pippin studied the map that Mungo had given her carefully. 'Along this tunnel and around that corner and we should be in this cavern here ... I think,' she whispered to Turbo. 'This is where Mungo thought they were digging and next to it is the chamber where we're going to trap Blowfart.'

Alan and Pippin hurried along the tunnel and sure enough, as they got closer, Pippin heard mining sounds.

Scrape, bang, ouch, clink!
Scrape, bang, ouch, clink!
Pass me that little spade,
Scrape, bang, ouch, clink!

Our heroes stopped, just as the tunnel opened out into a bigger chamber. They saw the large, flickering shadows of the poor mining creatures projected onto the wall by candlelight.

'Okay,' whispered Pippin, 'plan time. Muddy yourself up so you look like you've been digging here for nine weeks and five days.'

Pippin hid and Alan, now looking

grubby, snuck in amongst the miners. In his head, he counted to three, and then he shouted:

'I'VE GOT IT, I'VE GOT IT, EVERYONE! I'VE FOUND THE HUGE DIAMOND AND IT IS M to the A to the S-S-I to the V to the E to the MASSSSSIVE! We all have to go and tell Blowfart and then maybe he'll let us go! Quick, let's run!'

'Woo-hoo!' the animals all cheered as one.

'You lead the way,' Turbo said to a dusty little rabbit.

The miners were SO relieved and

happy – after so looong digging, it felt like years – they began to run out of the mines. They tore through the tunnels and were soon climbing the wooden stairs that led to Blowfart's lair.

'We found it!' screamed Alan as he skidded along the floor. 'I, Turbo, have found your diamond – oh yeah!!'

A pair of velvet curtains were thrown back and Blowfart slowly came out from behind them, his lab coat swishing as he walked. As far as they could tell, he was alone. Visbek was still strung up in his net in the the forest, like a sad sack of bad onions, and Gareth the mean cat was off doing whatever it is that evil cats do with their precious time off.

The Doctor approached Alan carefully and with a great deal of consideration he fixed his eyes on the little badger and attempted a bit of mind control. But clever Turbo Alan felt Blowfart's powerful mind trying to lock into his own, so he imagined looking directly at a huge diamond, to trick the Doctor. The little badger pictured the dazzle and the glare of the stupendous stone. It worked: Blowfart's eyes widened and silently he whispered, 'El Más Brillante. The moment has arrived.'

'C'mon, my lord,' Alan said to Blowfart. 'Follow me. I'll take you to it!'

As the plucky badger ushered the Doctor down towards the mines he looked over his shoulder and saw Martin nudge open the door to Blowfart's chamber. The brave stag had arrived to lead the forest animals to safety. Yay! Turbo winked at Martin, who grinned and waited until the coast was properly clear.

Back in the cave, Pippin heard the rumble of Mungo's explosion and checked her watch. She had ten minutes.

Blowfart heard it too. He stopped and looked at Alan. 'What was that?'

'Hopefully just the miserable forest collapsing into the mines,' replied Turbo, quick as a flash. 'Good riddance to the idiots, I say.'

'I'm beginning to like you, badger,' slithered Blowfart. 'You shall be semi-richly rewarded for this.'

I hope so, thought Turbo, smiling to himself and picturing some more dazzling sunshine as they rounded the last corner before the chamber where the miners had been working.

Pippin caught sight of them as she peeped out from behind her rock. Blowfart had a lantern with him – it dangled from the crook of his pointy elbow, swaying and creaking as he walked. She could see the cuddly-looking silhouette of her friend Turbo Alan and the angular silhouette of the evil Doctor.

The cold air of the cave got distinctly colder as Blowfart passed within a whisker of Pippin. The little girl trembled. She didn't even think she could *hold* a match, never mind light one. What on earth was she going to cock-a-doodle do?

'It's down there in the left-hand corner, my lord,' said the little badger. 'I'll let you go and have a moment on your own with it, so you can feel its magic wash over you.'

Blowfart's face lit up, the corners of his mouth twitched and he rubbed his tiny little hamster hands together and set off towards the darkest bit of the cave.

Turbo Alan tiptoed back to the entrance of the cave and hurried up to Pippin, who was curled up in a ball, wishing she had someone to help her.

Alan shook Pippin's trouser leg. 'Come on!' he urged. 'Light the fuse! Set off the dynamite!'

Hands shaking, Pippin picked out the matches from her pocket. She tried to light one on the wall of the cave – but it broke.

She tried another, dragging the match slowly and carefully across the cave wall.

That didn't work either.

She tried again and the same thing

happened, again and again. This was bad. Super-duper bad. She was running out of matches!

'Big pro-pro-problem,' she stammered. 'The cave walls are too cold and damp to light the matches.' It looked very much as though Pippin's world was about to crumble around her and she sank to her knees.

I'm sorry, my lovely readers, this is all too much for me. I don't think I can bear it. I am going to have to go and have a crisp sandwich and a glass of milk. Let's meet after that and maybe, just maybe, I will be able to funtinue this terribubbly bad section of the story.

Rough as a
Badger's Bottom

Pippin and Alan were in real trouble. Their plan to trap the evil Doctor underground was slipping away like a dog with a doughnut. They both froze as Blowfart's reptilian voice came from the depths of the cave.

'EL MÁS BRILLANTE. WHERE IS IT, BADGER? SHOW IT TO ME!'

Turbo was quick to reply. 'Ah, my lord, forgive me, I am only a badger – I always get my right mixed up with my left! It must be in the RIGHT-hand corner.'

'We only have seconds!' cried Pippin. 'We need something really rough to light this. It's the last match.'

'I KNOW!' said Turbo. 'Strike it on my little bum-bum – there's nothing rougher than a badger's booty. HERE!' And he stuck his rear high in the air.

I can do this, thought Pippin. She pictured her beloved Tony and she immediately grew a couple of inches taller and felt magical Shiny energy course through her. She struck the match hard against Turbo's posterior and it burst into a flame at once.

'Ouch!' squeaked Alan.

Pippin quickly lit the fuse, which began to splutter and sparkle and burn and fizz. She placed the dynamite in a crack in the rock above the cave entrance.

Blowfart's voice rang out again. 'BADGER – I DON'T SEE THE DIAMOND. COME AND SHOW ME.'

'I told you, it's there, my lord. It's about the size of a human head,' Alan shouted into the darkness.

'I DON'T SEE IT, BADGER! COME HERE IMMEDIATELY!!!'

'I'm coming, my lord, I will show you immediately ... Actually, on second thoughts, why don't you come up here and kiss my big rough badgery buttocks! OH YEAH!' (So rude.)

Turbo and Pippin now watched as Blowfart came hobbling back towards them at speed, lab coat billowing out behind him. His face was twisted with fury, but he was not quick enough. The beastly Doctor had run out of time. Pippin and Turbo dived behind a big rock and—

BOOM!

The dynamite exploded, bringing down a ton of rubble, completely sealing the Doctor inside the cave. Our heroic heroes could hear him ranting and raging and cursing on the other side of the rubble.

Pippin picked up Alan and gave him the biggest hug he had ever had. It was a hug fit for the king of the polar bears, which was lucky, because that was exactly what the little badger felt like.

As they hugged, plops of water started to drip from the ceiling of the cave. Then Pippin remembered her special friend. 'Tony!' she cried. 'Come on, Turbo, let's go!'

Pippin and Turbo sped through the tunnels and as they raced, the cave rain became heavier, dripping down in big fat muddy droplets.

'Looks like clever Mungo managed to blow up the dam,' grinned our hero as they sped along. Pippin looked over her shoulder – and her happiness turned to panic. A huge tidal wave was chasing them down the tunnel. She scooped up Alan and ran as fast as she could, leaping rocks and swerving around corners. Pippin was travelling so fast, she tripped and stumbled and almost fell – but managed to keep on her feet.

The powerful torrent was almost at her back now. They would be swallowed up by it within moments. They rounded a corner and reached the long staircase that led up into Blowfart's lair. Pippin kicked on with an extra burst of supersonic speed – and outran the rushing water. YAYY!!

They hurtled up the wooden stairs, ran and skidded into the central chamber of the lab and saw on Blowfart's desk that Gareth the mean cat was stuffed inside the cage that had once contained Tony. Sitting proudly on top was Tony, with his new best friend, Maria Oddplop. She was

coolly reading a very small book called *101 Fly Recipes*. Maria paused nonchalantly and looked up. 'Ah, *amigos*, it is good to see you!'

Pippin picked up the frog and hugged her, kissed her and put her on top of her head. 'Good to see you, Maria.' She looked at Gareth all caged up like an evil goose and added with a grin, 'Nice work!'

Finally, the moment she had been waiting for! Pippin turned to Tony and burst into tears. She lifted him up and kissed the top of his head. She hugged him and hugged him and hugged him again and they snuggled noses and Shined lovely warm messages of bright, brilliant, magical love to each other and, once more, the two of them felt complete.

'When my master gets back you are in big trouble!' meowed Gareth, through the bars.

Pippin turned and looked at the cat. 'He's not coming back,' she said. 'I think he will be sent to prison for a very long time. But I am going to let you go,' she continued, releasing him from the cage. 'Go back into the world, turn over a new leaf and be kind. And if you even THINK of trying any funny business, I will set Maria on you again.'

But the moment he was free, Gareth leaped up and scratched Pippin on the face so that she had three bloody claw marks on her cheek. What a horrible cat! Then he raced off into the depths of the laboratory.

Pippin didn't care. She felt whole again as she looked down at Tony peeping out of her pocket. She felt like everything was how it should be. Tony was back, right next to her heart, exactly where he belonged.

Yay! Now I'm feeling as nice as chutney. This is precisely how a chapter should end. I'm going to bed now. I'll tell you what happened next tomorrow.

Goodnighticus, sleep tighticus and mind the bed bugs don't biteicus.

The Party on the Top of the Hill

U p on the cliffs it had started to rain. Mungo the big, kind geologist stood on a rock next to the craggy cliff top above the mines and the lab, where they'd all planned to meet.

He and his helpers, Snape and Geoffrey, had been the first to arrive. They were soon followed by all the woodland animals who had not been part of the adventuring. They'd had enough time to pop back home to wash their little farmpits and have a quick game of Jenga.

They'd heard the underground explosion caused by Turbo and Pippin as they sealed the Doctor in the cave. Trees had wobbled and all the birds had flown into the sky, squawking madly. If you were Shiny or could understand Tweet, the international language of birds, you would have known they were all shrieking, 'Eek, what was that? Eek, what was that? Eek, what was that?'

Gradually the rest of the Shiny woodland gang began turning up. First were more birds, who landed in the trees around them, then came a few other creatures – otters, foxes, weasels and a giraffe. Haha! Not really a giraffe. I wanted to check if you were still glistening carefully and you were. Cool.

Next Martin the stag arrived triumphantly, surrounded by the miners he'd rescued from the lab. He was happy, but he couldn't help turning his mind to his father, Oswald. So much had happened – it felt like weeks since he'd seen the ancient, magical king of the deer.

Mungo looked over and saw sadness in the young stag's eyes. Walking over, he placed an arm around Martin and pulled him in for a man-hug. 'You did well, captain,' he said, smiling.

The animals sat quietly in the rain and waited. Half an hour passed. Everyone was afraid that Pippin's mission in the mines had ended badly.

Mungo peeled off from the group and looked into the distance. He was agitated and he kept checking his watch, even though he didn't wear one. Snape and

233

some of the other animals followed him, hoping for some sort of comfort. Snape looked at Mungo and baaaed up at him because she knew exactly what the big guy was thinking.

Mungo was hugely fond of little Pippin – she was like the kid sister he'd always wished he had, growing up. 'I'll never forgive myself if anything has happened to her. I love that little girl!' Mungo blurted out, his voice wobbly with sadness.

'And I love you!!!' said Pippin, appearing from the bushes just as Mungo was opening his heart to the little lamb.

The animals roared with joy and Mungo

picked up Pippin and danced and shrieked and shouted and wept because he was now officially the happiest man that had ever lived.

Everyone gathered round and a giant party began. There was a huge amount of dancing, cuddling and laughing in that happy scene on the top of the hill.

Then Maria the Spanish Ninja Frog Princess sprang up onto a big boulder and called everyone together. Pippin lovingly placed Tony next to the little frog. Then Maria shushed everyone so that Tony could make a speech.

'Those of you who know me know that

I am a mouse of very few words,' Tony began, 'so I will keep this brief. I would like to talk to you about my friend, Pippin – my SPECIAL friend. We have been on a scarifying journey together and for a while it looked like we wouldn't make it. But because of her bravery, I am free.'

'And woo-hoo for thaaaaat!' baaaed Snape. All the other animals laughed and shouted out their agreement.

When the joyous noise died down, Tony continued, 'I wanted Pippin to only ever talk to me. That was selfish and it almost cost us ALL very dearly.' Pippin looked at the crowd of animals all silently staring at her little mouse and her heart glowed with a million warm feelings of yummy nice. 'I wanted it to just be us forever,' Tony went on. 'But that was silly because we all need lots of friends and looking at you now, I understand that.'

Pippin smiled up at her special friend and the little mouse felt more loved than ever before. Tony continued: 'I want to say a big thank-you to Maria, to Mungo,

Martin, Alan, Snape and Geoff – but most of all I think we need to say a big thanks to Pippin – Shiny Pippin, the Shiniest Pippin in the whole of the world!'

Suddenly Maria GASPED very loudly and staggered backwards. She looked incredibly shocked. Everyone became silent and looked at the Frog Princess.

'THE SHINIEST!' she said.

'THE SHINIEST!

'Do you know what "Shiniest" is in Spanish?!'

Nobody had a clue. Everyone looked blank. Forest schools at best only taught a tiny bit of French.

Finally Maria said, 'Spanish for "the shiniest" is *el más brillante*! El Más Brillante is not a diamond, *amiga*. It is you! YOU are the thing that Blowfart was looking for . . .

You
ARE
El Más Brillante!'

There was silence on the top of the hill. Everyone stared open-mouthed at Maria and then at Pippin.

Then suddenly, from around the corner, came a sickeningly familiar sound.

'Hahahahahahahahahaha hahaha!'

Horrific horrid horror of all horrific horrid horrors – it was Blowfart and Gareth the cat. They looked like they had been to Hull and back and they had evil in their eyes.

Galactic
Electricity

The evil Doctor spoke in his vilest whisper. 'The Shiniest? The Shiniest? All these years I have been searching for a diamond that would increase my powers, but El Más Brillante

is not a diamond, Gareth – El Más Brillante
is a little girl!

'Hahahahahahahahaha hahahaha!

'You fools underestimated Gareth, my
clever cat companion. He's been hunting
rats in those underground tunnels for
months – he knew exactly how to find
me and get me out.' The fluffy white cat
smiled smugly, looked at Tony and licked
his lips.

The Doctor continued, 'You, Pippin,
will help me take my powers to the next
dimension. Excellent. Come with me. Very
generously, I will forgive that annoying little

incident down in the mine. Together we shall be unstoppable.'

Pippin looked straight at him. Gone was the fear she had felt in the mines. With the help of her friends, Pippin had grown in strength and in confidence.

'You are the meanest creature ever,' she said. 'I would rather die than come with you!'

The animals looked anxious. They all knew what the Doctor was capable of.

Blowfart looked at her with tiny piercing eyes. 'Normally I might grant that wish. But I suspect that to sap you of your powers, I will need you alive ...'

He began to move slowly and deliberately towards the little girl. Gareth sprang onto his back and curled around his shoulders, his face contorted into the smug, self-satisfied smile of an enormous meanie.

Suddenly the air began to crackle and sparkle and mixed in with it was the clatter of hooves as Granny burst through the bushes, riding on the back of Oswald the magnificent white stag.

'Yesss!' shouted Martin, and sprang to his father's side. Everybody cheered.

The Doctor glared at them. 'Well, if it isn't Margaret and her ridiculous fat white pony, Oswald the King of the Forest Idiots.

We meet again. Surely you know that you old fools are no match for me!'

'We'll see about that!' said Oswald, and wasting no time, he charged at the Doctor.

But Blowfart summoned all of his Shiny magic and formed a force field around himself. 'I am stronger than both of you put together! Your magic is certainly "interesting" but you are clearly just as weak as you ever were!' He channelled a ferocious bolt of energy that sent Granny and Oswald shooting backwards and they smashed into an old oak tree.

'I'm too old for this rubbish ...' said Oswald, staggering to his feet.

'Me too, muffin,' said Granny, dusting dirt off her shoulders and hoisting herself back up onto Oswald's back.

'Then maybe it's time to put you both out of your misery!' raged the Doctor, rolling up his sleeves and hobbling towards them with hate in his eyes.

Pippin felt a calmness descend upon her. She knew now that she was more magical with Tony next to her heart, that she was stronger with her new friends by her side and that Granny and Oswald were more powerful when they fought together. So it made sense that for maximum power, she and Tony should be with Granny and Oswald. Together they would be a force to be reckoned with.

With Tony in her pocket, she ran towards the huge white stag, leaped up and joined her granny on the great warrior's back. And in that moment she truly realised who she was: in that moment, she *BECAME* El Más Brillante.

The air sizzled with galactic electricity – it was as if Pippin was at the centre of an enormous solar storm. She closed her eyes and focused all of her and Tony's Shiny powers through Oswald. They all became one and ancient and brilliant starlight radiated out of them. It blinded Blowfart as he backed away.

'If you strike me down, I shall just come back again and again and **again**. You have NO **IDEA** how powerful I have become,' Blowfart proclaimed.

'Well, we don't *want* to strike you down!' said Pippin. 'We just want you to stop being mean.'

Oswald looked at the evil Doctor. 'We may not know how powerful you have become. But I think you underestimate how powerful *we have always been*!' The huge white stag put his head down and sprang into a gallop. Once more, Granny and Pippin and Tony concentrated all their Shiny magic through the stag's powerful body – and Oswald kicked the evil Doctor right in the centre of his chest.

This magic was too much for Blowfart and Gareth. With a terrible cry, they both exploded into a million tiny black, silver and golden sparkles and the air crackled and fizzed just like it had done many years earlier when the star had exploded.

Chubby the magpie swooped in and out of the sparkles, gobbling as many of them as possible into his tummy for safekeeping, until the last one fizzed, spluttered and finally went out.

An explosion of cheers rang out from the gathered woodland creatures. Granny hugged Pippin like mad and Mungo came over and put his huge geologist's arms around them both. Then all the other animals came over and joined in a big group hug. And right at the centre of it was El Más Brillante – and, in her pocket, little Tony, smiling like a monkey in a banana factory.

You Should Always Keep in Touch with Your Friends

After their enormous hug-a-doodle, Pippin, Granny, Oswald, Mungo and all the other creatures (great and small) slowly made their way back home through the forest.

Little Turbo Alan the badger went back to his field with Snape the lamb. 'Thank you both so much,' said Pippin, as they left 'I couldn't have done it without you!' Turbo blushed and tripped over and Snape very loudly baaaed a long lamby laugh.

At Oswald's Well they stopped for a drink. Maria the Frog Princess climbed down off Pippin's head and said, 'See you later, *amigos*! El Más Brillante – you did good!'

'You did good too, little Maria Oddplop!' Pippin beamed.

Tony climbed down Pippin's trouser leg and scuttled over to Maria. 'Thank you, Maria. You have changed my life. I don't know how I can thank you for what you have done for us. We will come and see you soon. Promise.'

Maria smiled and dusted something invisible off each of her little green shoulders. 'It was nothing, *amigo*. You are a very brave mouse.'

Tony blushed. He had never thought he would hear *anyone* call him brave.

At last they reached Granny's house. Chubby spotted something sparkly and flew up into a tree to investigate. Oswald and Granny said a fond goodbye to each other and vowed that they would see each other much more often from now on.

Pippin stroked Martin's head. She pulled him in for a cuddle and kissed him on his soft nose. 'Thank you,' she said. Martin smiled. Then he and his father walked slowly off into the woods, with Oswald telling his son that there was a large piece of comfy moss under an oak tree with his name on it and he was planning to relax and do nothing until forever o'clock.

That left Mungo, Pippin, Tony and Granny. So they all went inside Granny's cottage and put the kettle on. While Mungo and Granny had a big cup of tea and got to know each other, Pippin and Tony climbed up onto Granny's comfy pink sofa and made themselves very comfortable. They ate Monster Munch, snuggled and watched snooker's most ridiculous star, Donnio Sillyman, on Granny's enormous tellywision until they fell asleep and began to dream: Tony about hazelnuts and

Babybels and Pippin about having amazing adventures in the woods with a big gang of lovely animal friends.

And that, my delightful little chums, is

THE ALMOST END

How I Wonder What You Are

Yes, that, dearest readers, is pretty much it. The water and funtimes were restored to Funsprings. A local and very wealthy none-of-your-businessman, Sir Aslan Ragu, was so pleased that he rewarded Pippin with fifty gazillion pounds, which she spent very funwisely.

She bought Granny a jetpack to help her get around more easily. She gave some money to her favourite geologist, who promptly bought an enormous bag of fancy rocks to study and an old fire engine, which he converted into an ice-cream van and parked in the square in the middle of town.

They gave Granny's old cellar a spring clean and a lick of paint and decided to use it as the headquarters for a new crime-solving business. Pippin employed Tony, Snape, Turbo, Chubby, Maria Oddplop and some of the otters – gaah, I mean the OTHERS! One last typing blundergaffe for the road, my friends. I am sorry for all of my weird and wonky writing.

You will be glad to hear that over the years they all had a great many exciting gladventures and one or two very terribubble badventures. Perhaps I will tell you about them some time – *if you are good*. However, if you come round my house and eat up all my chutney and fart in my study, you can forget it.

THE PROPER END

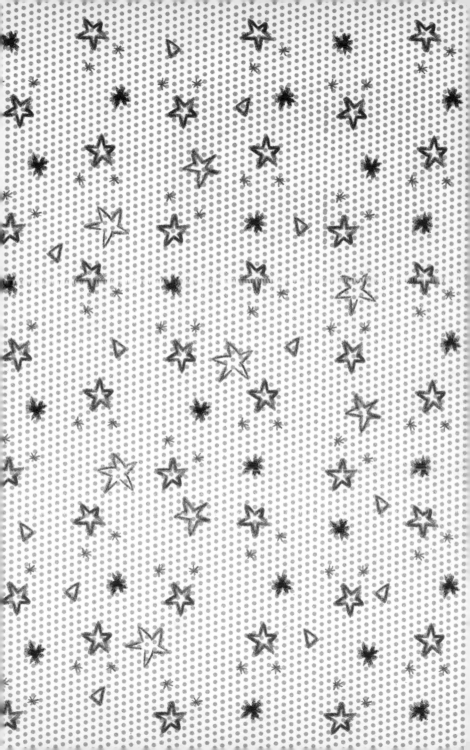

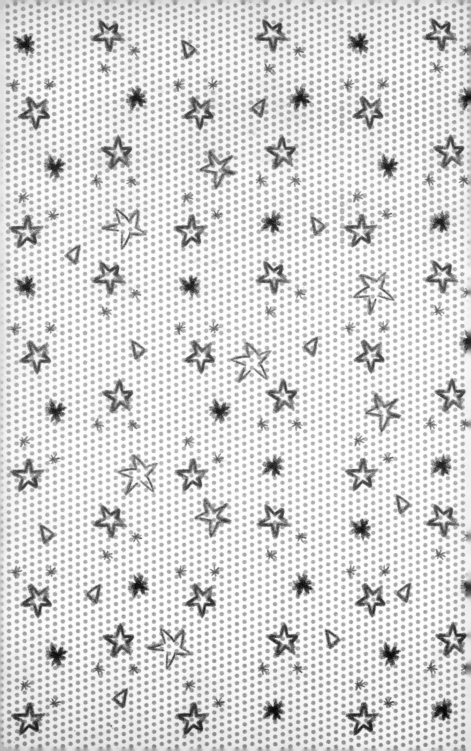